Infiltrating Her Pack

Black Hills Wolves

By

Dominique Eastwick

Infiltrating Her Pack

Published by Decadent Publishing Company, LLC

Look for us online at:

www.decadentpublishing.com

Also by Dominique Eastwick

Strawberry Kisses
The Duke and the Virgin
The Marquis and the Mistress
The Earl and His Virgin Countess
The Viscount and the Virgin
Shifting Hearts
Siren's Serenade
Healing His Soul's Mate

Dedication

Special thanks to Rebecca Royce for thinking enough
of my writing to allow me to play in her world ☺
To T.t and Toni for loving my books as much as I do.
As always, thank you to Nadine who pushes me to stop
procrastinating.

Chapter One

Silence—complete and utter silence.

Z stood for a moment, allowing it to roll through him. Ah, the familiar atmosphere of hostility and distrust. Nothing new, and exactly the way he liked it. If a room full of wolves suddenly gained a trust or desire to be in his presence, then they knew more about him than he wanted them to know, and more than was safe. One by one, the customers at the tables in the old, rustic honky-tonk in Los Lobos began to chatter, lower in volume, more intense in conversation than moments earlier.

"Welcome back, Z." Gee, the owner and pack historian, waved in greeting without even glancing in his direction when Z approached the bar. But then, the barkeep didn't need to look up to know who'd entered his establishment with that kind of reception. Had the room yelled Z's name, it wouldn't have been as effective as the deafening silence that always greeted his return. No one knew anything about him other than his name—Z.

Just Z.

As much as he would have preferred to head

straight to the room he'd rented, social etiquette demanded he at least say hello to his landlord. Z placed the large, plain cardboard box he carried on the scarred wood surface between them and waited, knowing the bear-shifter could hold out only so long.

Gee lifted his head from what he had been doing and licked his lips. In a voice so low even Z had to strain to hear, he asked, "Is that what I think it is?"

"Why not open it and find out?" Z pushed the box a little closer.

Gee took a step. As he reached out to touch the package, he paused and glared at Z. "It's not another one of those blasted beeswax candles, is it?"

"No, no candles. You didn't like the candle, I take it?" To be honest, Z hadn't known what to do with the candle, but the store owner had given it to him for free when he'd bought one of each of her varieties of honey. So, he thought maybe the guy could burn it or give it to his daughter as a present.

"Do you have any idea how long it took me to get the wax out from between my teeth?" Baring them, Gee growled.

"You ate it!"

"Would you lower your damned voice?" He searched the room to ensure no one noticed them before focusing on the box once again. "It smelled like honey, and I was...out."

"Out? There were twenty-four plastic teddy bear bottles in that case." Z couldn't help himself—he threw his head back and howled with laughter. He laughed until his sides hurt, and when Gee punched his arm to get him to stop, it only drove his amusement further. Again the customers hushed, no one there having ever seen any human side of Z. Only Gee had, and only when the two would meet over drinks and cards. Gee said something to the bar which Z couldn't make out over his own chuckles.

"You need help, bear, like rehab help." Z pulled out an example as evidence. "As you can see, it's all thick, golden-sweet honey."

Gee licked his lips again before grabbing the container and holding it close to his chest. "Will you lower your voice?" he demanded again.

"What are you afraid of? Your secret will get out that you have a serious addiction to the sweet stuff?"

"I would prefer to avoid being compared to Winnie the Pooh, if you please."

"Your secret is safe with me." Closing the box, Z tapped the top. "Can I get a beer?"

"What would you like?" Gee asked, opening the

top again and lifting out each honey jar then running a rough finger over the homemade labels before replacing them gingerly.

"Is there a choice?"

"Not really, but you can choose which cooler I get it from."

"Seriously, man, you have to do something to improve this bar. Even if it is the only place in the town, have some self-respect, some pride."

"People like things the way they are." Gee cradled the case like a baby. "North Carolina?" he asked, referring to the *Made in NC* labels.

"Yeah, good barbeque and sweet tea that would make even a healthy person diabetic."

No one but Drew, the Alpha of the pack, had a clue where Z headed at any given time. Perhaps Drew's Enforcer, Ryker, might, but as the Enforcer and Z didn't talk much, Z had no idea what information Ryker had on him as a pack Infiltrator. And if he did, Ryker wouldn't talk. So Gee had come to rely on the honey as his way of tracking where Z had been.

"Here is your beer. The linens are where they have always been. And feel free to join me for dinner tonight if you're in the mood."

"We shall see. Of course, you might be in the grip

of a honey coma by then."

"You might be right. And in that case, you'll have to run the bar."

Z snorted, grabbed his beer, and took the stairs to the second floor.

"Oh yeah, and Drew wants to see you as soon as you get into town," Gee yelled at his back.

So much for getting some rest. Z rubbed his face and steeled his shoulders. Turning right at the landing, he strolled the length of the upper floor, only stopping at the linen closet to retrieve a set of clean, yellowed-with-age sheets. The floor below returned to its normal hum, the stranger already forgotten. At the very end of the landing, he paused at the last door, ensuring the safeguards he had put in place were still intact then opened it.

Z chanted under his breath until a soft glow illuminated the charms and they came to life before crumbling into a pile of dust as his feet. Brushing it aside with the tip of his boot, he crossed the threshold, convinced the room hadn't been disturbed since he'd left it three-and-a-half weeks before. He trusted Gee, Drew, and even Ryker, but he had no reason to trust anyone else in the Tao Pack any more than they trusted him. For that reason, ensuring even an empty

5

room remained untouched had to be of the utmost importance.

He dropped both the sheets and his bag on the twin bed before crossing to the window, repeating the same ritual from the door before he could open it. Taking a swig of his beer, he watched the people along the dusty main street. Bit by bit, the small town and pack were repairing and healing. It would be years before they could move on from the evil grasp of their former Alpha, Magnum, but Drew, the new pack leader, exceled so far where his father had failed.

Breathing in the fresh air, Z evaluated the old town. A few buildings showed signs of some TLC. Progress might be slow, but progress nonetheless. He stretched with a jaw-popping yawn. He yearned to jump into the small bed in the corner, wanting—no, *needing* to get some serious sleep. Weeks had passed since his head had rested on a pillow under the roof of someone he trusted. He had spent weeks sleeping with one eye open and an ear peeled for the slightest thing. Although the people here didn't trust him, he trusted Gee, and he could let his guard down...if only a little.

A female beta strolled along the road alone below the bar. Z also smelled, though they were not in his line of sight, two young males following her in the distance. But he couldn't sense any spike in testosterone to warn him the female might be in danger. The boys showed no interest in her at the moment.

Closing the window, he turned back to the room. He cocked his head, inhaled and relaxed. Then with the next breath, shifted. Unlike most Wolves, whose change from human to wolf form could take some time, Z and all his kind had the ability to shift from one second to the next.

He brushed against the metal bed frame, then the old wood chair, leaving his scent heavy in the room. Anyone on the second floor would smell his presence, even the most dimwitted of Wolves. Convinced anyone foolish enough to search for him would believe he remained in the room, Z gave his fur one last shake, removing the last of the scent with it.

He left and, once on the landing, closed his eyes to locate each of the individuals in the bar below. The only human appeared to be in the kitchen, not the main hall, which made his escape much easier, and the Bear remained too focused on his new case of honey to care. The problem with Wolves, and most shifters for that matter, they'd long ago stopped relying on their sight and let their sense of smell alert them to danger.

Humans, however, did the opposite—relying on sight and forgetting to follow their nose. Humans would believe what they saw over what they smelled. Z had witnessed it recently, when humans dismissed a wolf at a party as a figment of too much champagne.

As expected, Z slipped undetected out of the bar and right out the front door with no one the wiser. He took the long way around the center of town to get to Drew's office, wanting to assess any weaknesses the Alpha and his Enforcer might have missed. They were doing a great job, but sometimes it took an outside set of eyes to see flaws in procedures. And as an Infiltrator, no one could do the job better than Z. If he couldn't get through a security checkpoint, no one could.

The Infiltrators were much like the ninjas of myths. Some believed they didn't exist and most who knew about them didn't live long enough to tell. Tallying the mental list of items to talk to Drew about, Z entered the old barn. Skirting the edges, he avoided any sign of anyone. Drew had made good strides repairing the neglect his father's reign had played on the pack. Approaching the battered door to the room Drew used for an office, Z listened and smelled before comfortable turning the corner through the crack in the door and into the office.

Z made it halfway into the room before the Alpha paused in his paperwork, sniffed the air as if sensing something amiss. Good sign. The other times Z had done this very exercise, Drew had shown no acknowledgement of the Infiltrator's presence. Word should be reaching him soon about the strange wolf's reappearance in town.

As if on cue, Ryker, the pack Enforcer, stormed into the office, bristling with unspent fury.

"He's returned." The large man crossed his arms, blocking the door.

"He?" Drew didn't stop working on the papers before him.

"Z."

The Alpha placed his pen down and faced his Enforcer. "Good. I've been anticipating his return, though not for another week."

"I don't trust him."

"You don't trust most."

"I trust him and his kind even less."

Z shifted unnoticed and slid from his place in the corner, prepared for Ryker's attack should the Enforcer feel a desire to vent his spleen on his head when he realized the bane of his existence had been in the room. "A wise decision," he said. "My kind should never be fully trusted."

Drew rose, prepared to stop a fight. "Damn it, Z, don't antagonize him."

Z, who stood a few inches shorter than the two men, simply shrugged. "It's a part of my charm."

"Charm, my ass. Both of you have a seat."

Although Drew wasn't his Alpha, Z followed the request nonetheless. Dour and brooding, Ryker took a seat. The man might not have a great deal of friends, but he happened to be one of the most well-respected Enforcers alive. He held true to his blood oaths and somehow managed to protect the pack from the madness of the previous Alpha the best he could. That being said, getting into a fight with the man whose fists were the size of ham hocks did not rank on Z's to-do list.

Obviously gauging the chance of violence between the two wolves, he asked, "What do you have for me?"

"The Smoky Mountain packs have no idea where Malcolm's rejects are. I did trace two to an area outside Boone, North Carolina. I have some trackers on it, but they're deep in the forest bed, and those woods are dense. It might take some time, but they will come into town somewhere, and my ladies will be there when they do."

"And the threat from the pack in Georgia?"

"Confirmed, but at the moment, that pack doesn't know its nose from its ass and is chasing its own tail."

"You're doing, I take it?"

"I can neither confirm nor deny my involvement."

"So, I shouldn't expect their Alpha demanding to challenge Drew anytime soon?" Ryker asked.

Shaking his head, Z focused his attention on his adversary. "I'll make another pass through there in a few weeks, but they have other fish to fry at the moment closer to home. Coming out this way would leave them open to attack from other packs."

Drew leaned back in his chair, lacing his fingers behind his head, and took a deep breath. "What did you think of the improvements to town?" He didn't mean the new coat of paint on the general store.

"I was impressed. It took me a good hour to get through the patrols. They're more observant. But, they need to shake things up. By watching for an hour, I saw their security pattern and slipped in. I suggest randomizing it a bit."

"Did you hide your scent?"

"I did not."

"So, how do we keep your kind out?" Ryker asked.

"You can't. But if you would teach those damned pups to open their eyes and not their nostrils, you would have a slight bit more luck. Otherwise, I recommend a human on patrol every now and then."

The Enforcer simply growled.

"It's harder to fool both races at once. The other issue is the safety of your women. I walked right next to a group, gave off the air of an aggressive male, and not one took notice."

"It's a fine line between letting everyone breathe easily and keeping them on their guard." Drew wiped a hand over his weary face.

"That is why I have no desire to ever fall in my father's footsteps and be Alpha."

"Your dad is Alpha?" Little shocked Drew, but Z's comment had his head snapping up. But then Z rarely spoke of his pack to anyone.

"He is, but succession is voted on in my pack."

"Interesting. I was unaware of that. Seems far more civilized than I expected." Drew smiled. "I failed your test again when you snuck in."

"You didn't pass, but you didn't fail. You knew something was off. You looked around. That's a huge step. I doubt I'll be able to fool you again."

When Z had first met Drew, the wolf had been

angry, alone, and desperate, the metal storage shed he'd lived out of the only protection from the oncoming full moon. Drew was dependent on the full moon and forced to shift. Z, having been born moon-dependent, could still remember the pain, even a century on, of defying his nature to shift. Infiltrators possessed a mutant gene that allowed them, with due diligence, to alter their need and abilities to shift. With a great deal of initial pain, patience, and force from the elders in his pack, he'd eventually broken his lunar connection.

Infiltrators' ability to discern a person's character had been bred in them and a key to their ability to stay alive. Immediately, Z had seen the honor of the younger Drew. Well-informed on the chaos of his former pack, Z had searched Drew for the signs of madness his father, Magnum, had become infamous for. Z had been charged with checking in on the young wolf from afar. But after watching Drew deal with a full moon, Z could no longer stay in the distance.

Over the years, he'd met with Drew, making sure the man had whatever help he would accept, all the while establishing his sanity or lack thereof. The Infiltrators wanted to keep track of Drew as the Tao Pack rapidly descended into its downward spiral. None of which Z informed Drew of, since it was against the code of Z's pack to interfere with what the Fates dished out. Infiltrators could defend, they could scout, and in extreme cases, fight, but their main goals were to act as information recon.

That's not to say Z hadn't done his fair share of screwing with people's heads or diverting them from what they were focused on. Those out to attack the Tao Pack while they were still unable to completely defend themselves were treated to a good mind-fuck. And like most Infiltrators, Z could always find the loopholes in any code of law but one—if someone was in trouble, he would be the first to step in and help; however, in matters of pack affairs where the Alpha required being taken out, he could do nothing. That code had no loophole and met with swift and absolute punishment.

"I have another job if you want it."

"I have nothing else pressing at the moment." Z's pack wanted him to check-in in person, but that could wait another few weeks. If anything critical happened, they would have told him when he'd checked in via phone earlier in the week. Although, he really would have preferred to take a week off to sleep.

"I still can't afford to pay you."

"I have not asked for anything but a room." Which

he'd paid for, but Drew didn't know that. He, at least, could feel he'd paid Z that much. "Besides, one day I might ask a favor."

Drew pulled a file from his desk drawer. "A week ago I had a visit from a Ripley Greystone of the Greystone Pack."

"Greystone?" There were few packs Z's kind didn't have knowledge of. "I have never heard of them."

"Neither had I." Drew pushed an eight-by-ten profile picture of a blonde woman toward him. "She came to me, seeking protection for her pack."

Z jerked his head in the direction of the Enforcer. "Seems more his area than mine."

"Normally, yes. But when a beautiful woman, *very* beautiful, and physically strong comes seeking help from a pack still rebuilding, my hackles go up."

"Strong how?" Z glanced from the file folder before him.

"She's one of the strongest women I have seen. I observed her help one of our pack. She lifted a rock that would have taken two of our males to raise then placed it under the wheel of a wagon as if it were nothing."

"So, why would a beta this tough be in need of protection?"

"Exactly. If the betas were that strong, what must their dominants or Alpha be like? And why send a woman to do your dirty work?"

"Suspicious."

"Gee has nothing to say on the subject or the pack except he thought they had died out decades ago."

"So you fear this might be a way to divide your resources."

Ryker sneered. "Or infiltrate our town."

Z surveyed the picture again. She didn't have the appearance of a muscular beast, but her beauty made him pause. "How big is the pack?"

"She wouldn't say, so no idea, and she wouldn't say why she sought out our protection either."

"Were you supposed to take her at her word?"

"Apparently." Drew tapped his desk. "I told her without more information I couldn't be of help. She seemed to accept it, even thanked me for my time, but as she turned, I saw her despair. In that moment, a wave of her hopelessness crashed over me, and something else, too."

"What else?" Z fought the urge to look over the picture again. He'd never taken a second glance at a target before, and he didn't want to draw attention to his odd attraction to the woman in a photo or give in to the bizarre urge to stroke the black-and-white image of her face.

"Fear." Drew stood and walked to the small window that faced out to the main street. "Her fear grabbed me and has gnawed at me since she left. I can't sleep until I know this woman isn't in a situation my pack once faced. I left my mate to the misery of one crazed man. I can't leave another female that way."

"No matter what I find, I can't take out their Alpha."

"And I'm not asking that of you." Drew turned to Z. "Tell me what's going on, so I can make a more informed decision."

"I'll leave in the morning."

"Check with Gee. He might give you some information."

"I thought you said he didn't tell you anything."

"He didn't, but I'm not an Infiltrator, and I do not have whatever secret weapon you seem to have in your arsenal. Care to share what that secret is?"

"Not on your life, Alpha." Standing to exit, Z patted the Enforcer's shoulder. "Always good chatting with you, Ryker. Drew, you will know something when I do."

Once outside the barn, Z located a signal for his

cell phone—not always easy in the isolated town. Opening his pack's secure search engine, he searched for Ripley Greystone. Immediately, genealogy and family-tree sites jumped on the screen. He scanned through the images. Surprised with what came up, he enlarged a picture associated with a blog post on a travel site about a whitewater rafting tour trip. A grainy cell phone picture of friends accompanied the article, and in the background stood Ripley. If she was a rafting guide, it explained the whys and hows of her physical strength. But, if her pack as a whole was unusually strong, that also explained the choice to be river guides. So that didn't answer a single one of his questions.

Next he searched the rafting company.

Shaking his head, he drummed the photos. "It can't be that easy." For a pack that had fallen off the face of the planet, they were hiding in plain sight. *Grey Wolf River Tours*. Not one picture of Ripley Greystone graced their website, though. So, Z dialed the number provided as he made his way back to Gee's.

"Grey Wolf River Tours, how can I help you?" a man's voice vibrated in his ear.

It didn't go unnoticed to Z that the man didn't offer a name. Adopting an air of ignorance, Z answered, "Um, yes, a friend of mine recommended you guys."

"That's great, we love hearing that." An air of pride filled the man voice. "What level of rafter are you?"

"This would be my first experience rafting."

"Not a problem, everyone has to start somewhere. Okay, let's see…I have a few questions. When are you looking to be in the area, and how many are in your party?"

"I will actually be close this weekend, and it's only me."

"Just you?" Suspicion laced the man's words.

Shit. Z paused mid-step. *Time to change tack.* "My buddy wants to do a five-day rafting tour, but I would hate to get out on the water and realize I suffer from seasickness, or worse, hated rafting altogether. I thought I would check out your overnight trip. That way, when I go out with my friend later on, I'm not such a dork on the water."

"I totally get it, dude."

The distrust eased as the guy laughed. Z suspected he was dealing with an omega. Relieved, he continued to work his way down Main Street as he made his reservations.

"Let's see, we have a few slots open for the weekend overnight."

"Fantastic. My name is Zames with a Z." The fake name rolled off his tongue without thought. Each Infiltrator out in the field adopted a full name to prevent raising suspicions. He gave the rest of the information requested, then said, "Oh, I know it's a long shot, but my buddy said his guide had been called Raleigh."

"Raleigh? Oh, you must mean Ripley. She isn't the guide for this weekend's tour, but you'll be happy with any of our guides."

Ending the call, Z immediately texted his sister, N, who headed the pack-history information center. N, like all Infiltrators, bore only a letter, number, or symbol as her name. *A* being the Alpha and *B* his beta. When a new Alpha would be voted in, he would take on the new letter-name, as would his mate, opening their old symbols for new pups.

Z: *N, any and all information on the Greystone Pack of the Grey Wolf River as soon as possible.*

Entering the bar, he ignored the silence and walked straight over to Gee. "Offer still on the table for dinner and drinks?"

"You come seeking information?" Gee headed for

the back door, and Z followed. "This about that girl who came into town hoping for some help?"

When they were settled at the picnic table located behind the kitchen, Z said, "Greystone Pack."

"Honestly, I thought the pack died off decades ago. They went from being prominent to forgotten in a few years."

"Prominent how?"

"Large, powerful, but not malicious or cruel."

The waiter brought their food. Z looked down at the burger, his hunger overruling the lack of desire for the food set before him. Of course, the options were limited at the bar—hamburgers or hamburgers, and on some nights, cheeseburgers.

Once the omega moved safely out of earshot, Gee continued, "Last I remember hearing, their Alpha had died, but I never heard who took over. Never thought about it until now."

"How did they make their living, do you remember?" Z asked.

"Fishing. No—rafting tours, I think. Odd choice, but who am I to say how anyone should make a living? At least they aren't hurting anyone, right?"

Z's phone pinged and he glanced at it. The text message from N couldn't wait. "Excuse me, I've got to take this."

Gee waved him on, his mouth full of burger.

N's message glowed at him.

N: *Nothing Z...absolutely nothing*

Fuck. Just as he'd suspected.

Z: *Thanks for checking*.

No sooner had he hit send, N's next message appeared.

N: *A wants you to infiltrate and get the information back for the keeper's files*.

Z looked at the sky. What the hell did they think he'd been doing? Instead of telling his sister this wasn't his first rodeo, he typed instead.

Z: *On it. Last known Alpha died forty years ago, and now the pack runs a rafting company. All I know*.

N: *Figured you were. When are you coming home? I miss my big brother*.

Z: *Soon*.

A lie, and she would know that.

N: *Right. Heard that before. Be safe*.

Z: *Always am*.

He hit the delete button, and the conversation disappeared. "My keepers know nothing."

"Well, that makes me feel better." Gee lifted his beer and laughed.

Chapter Two

Ripley hated paperwork—the bills and the accounting—but more than anything she hated being stuck inside. She longed to be on the river, in the woods, running in wolf form—running free. At the moment, she couldn't do any of those things. Throwing her pencil on her desk, she stomped to the window. Her sisters were dealing with the rafts, going out and helping to load the trailer for the tourist trip this afternoon.

The door opened, and Janey, her youngest sister, came in rubbing a bandana over the back of her neck. "That's it for today. Last two boats for the rapid tours have gone out, and the overnight passengers should be rolling in very soon. I don't ever remember a summer this busy."

"Business is definitely good." Silver lining to the fact their pack currently fought off serious issues with a coyote band. "Perhaps now we can hire some protection."

"Do you really think it calls for that?"

"I don't know, but I don't trust the *coyotes*." For

years, the coyotes had tried to woo or bring Ripley's pack and their band together. Over the last few years, the rebuffs of their advances on her pack had been met with hostility, and lately, though Ripley couldn't prove the coyotes were the culprits, violence. Nothing had occurred that, on its own, had caused more than a raised eyebrow, but put together with her suspicions, it made her nervous for her pack. Small things like dead animals left on the steps of their business, a billboard vandalized, missing oars and small punctures in one of the rafts.

A new, pristine black SUV pulled into the guest parking lot, and a tall, fashionable man stepped out, stretched, and smelled the air. The hackles on her nape rose. Not only did the man seem out of place—too high-style for their usual clientele—but he could have come right off the cover of GQ.

"Janey, how many are in tonight's overnight?"

Peeking around the office refrigerator door, Janey pulled the water jug out and started to refill her tin water bottle. "Two families who are friends, apparently. They vacation every year together. And a guy who called two days ago."

"Alone?"

"Yeah."

"That didn't raise any alarms with anyone?"

Unfortunately, Ripley seemed to be the only one who saw the world as dangerous and the people in it not always kind.

"Walter questioned the man about why he would want to come rafting and camping alone."

"And?" Why could no one give information freely?

"And his explanation appeared logical to Walter."

Walter, one of the many omegas in the pack, covered the office weekdays and took the reservations. He would accept anything, no matter what someone told him. His kind heart couldn't see that any person would have a reason to be less than who they said they were. Ripley wasn't so understanding or gullible. She couldn't afford to be— she had the pack safety to think about.

The door opened and the human male's cologne scent hit her senses like a wall of steam, making it hard to catch her breath. Her nipples hardened as long-dormant hormones jolted awake. Closing her eyes, she let an overwhelming sexual attraction wash through her. She gripped the counter, hoping to gain control. If he noticed her response to him, he showed no sign of it. He didn't even glance in her direction.

"Welcome. Can I help you?" Janey's voice, usually

high and perky, dropped into a husky tone as she flirted with the stranger. Although it shouldn't have bothered Ripley, for the first time, her sister's svelte, bombshell body with full breasts *did* bother her.

The man lifted his sunglasses and placed them on top of his head, then dealt Janey a full-out, killer smile. Teeth, perfect and white, gleamed behind full, kissable lips. "I hope so. I called about the overnight excursion tonight."

"You must be Zames?" Janey leaned in, emphasizing her cleavage while pushing a clipboard over. "Read this and sign the waiver, here and here. If you have any questions, please don't hesitate to ask."

Grabbing the pen and clipboard, tall-dark-and-gorgeous took himself to the bench. Most people glanced over the waiver and rules, but he seemed to read every word before signing a Z with flourish on the two areas she had indicated.

"I'm not the only one going tonight, am I?"

"Nah, the rest of the group hasn't arrived yet. They should be here anytime," Janey said.

"While you're waiting, if you have any food for the coolers, we can get into the boat and I can get you a dry sack." Ripley ignored her sister's questioning gaze. The rule had always been if you brought it, you packed it. But she couldn't trust her instincts with this man. Granted, those same instincts were telling her to rip his clothes off and ride him until she couldn't walk. "Those your bags right next to your vehicle?"

"Yes." Passing the waiver back to Janey, Zames trailed fast on Ripley's heels as she went outside then headed her off by a step, lifting the backpack. He followed her to the riverbed. "Should I pack my cell phone away, too?"

For a moment, looking into his green eyes, she found it difficult to remember what they were talking about. "Um...cell phone. You only need to put it in the dry pack if you want to. Your trip today is very calm but picturesque. Most people like to take some photos to remember the experience. You might get a little wet, but there isn't much of a chance of falling out unless you jump or decide to take a swim."

"I promise not to jump."

"Always a good idea, and your guide will let you know where it's safe to swim should you so choose." She pulled out one of the black wet packs, which resembled a large bag made of tire rubber. "Anything you want out of that?" she asked, reaching for his backpack. It was imperative she touched it.

Handing it over to her, he shook his head and

turned as two large *Travel America* RVs rolled in, and a boisterous lot of pre-teens jumped out. "The party has arrived."

"Good luck. You might want to jump after all." She rolled the top of the bag until it had a tight seal. Making room in the motorboat filled with the coolers and supplies for the night's camping, she put the bag in the front with enough room for the other ones to come. "Grab a life vest. And we sell beer inside. You might want to grab a six-pack. Otherwise, your guide will be here shortly. Enjoy your trip."

After briefly greeting the new arrivals, Ripley made her way back to the main building.

Before she could enter, her sister hissed in her ear. "What in the hell was that all about? Since when do we help anyone with their gear, and why are you putting your scent all over it?"

Jealousy, unlike Ripley had ever felt, ripped through her. "Worried I'm going to step into your territory?"

"What the hell are you talking about?" Her sister sniffed before throwing her hands in the air. "What has gotten into you? You're acting like a lunatic."

What *was* she doing? Why did she feel this hostility? It wasn't like Ripley at all. Rolling her neck until it cracked, she took a deep breath. "You're right, I am not myself. I don't trust him. Something about him isn't quite what it seems."

"And maybe you're seeing a boogeyman where there is none."

"Perhaps, although I need to go through his gear just in case. But I can't have him know that, so I touched it in case he smells me on it after I go through it."

"He's human. He wouldn't have had a clue."

"I'm not so sure."

That got her sister's attention. "Did you smell something? I couldn't, other than the heady cologne made especially for him."

"No, the lack of other smells worried me. Unless the man lives in an animal-slash-plant-free zone and never comes across anything of nature, then he must live in a bubble."

"Perhaps he took a shower."

Oh, dear heaven. Images of him naked standing under jets of water forced Ripley to squeeze her thighs together. "Trust me, please."

"What are you thinking? Coyote?"

"If he is, he's the best-looking, well-groomed one I have ever seen." Understatement of the century. He was the kind of man T-shirts clung to like a woman wished she could. "Look at him. No coyote could afford to live the way he does, and they certainly couldn't hire him."

"So, what's the plan?"

"Albert will take the boat and supplies out to the camp. I'll meet him upstream, go through the bag long before the other boat gets even close, and will have some answers that way."

"Geez, Ripley, do you really think he's a threat?"

A definite threat to her, if not the pack. The attraction to him bothered her on a level nothing else could. And that he seemed oblivious to it *and her* didn't help her disposition. "I don't know, but I'm not willing to bet the pack's safety on him being only some guy."

"Some sexy guy."

Done with the conversation and her pesky sister at the moment, Ripley changed course. "Janey, I think you have a tour to guide."

"Oh crap, you're right," she yelped, grabbing the keys to the old school bus they used to collect the rafters after their adventure through the rapids. "Be careful."

"Careful is my middle name," Ripley mumbled to

herself.

Once in her office, she watched as the coolers and the dry packs were loaded into the old red outboard motorboat. The mystery man, whose name according to the paperwork was Zames Smith, chatted with the other tourists before getting in the raft and moving toward the rear. Ripley suspected he'd moved back there to interrogate Eric, his guide. God love Eric. He might be strikingly gorgeous, but although the lights were on, no one was home, so any conversation Zames thought to have with him would be sadly lacking.

Albert waved to the group and said something that made the people in the raft chuckle before he roared off to the meeting point. Taking the side door out, Ripley headed into the wooded area behind the building. Once convinced she couldn't be seen, she shifted. The short electric shock followed by cracking bones flooded pain through her then faded away just as quickly. Shifting sucked but a necessity in her life.

She followed the raft for an hour, observing from the safety of the river brush, until she finally stepped out, curious what Zames would do if he saw a wolf. He glanced her way several times, well aware of her presence. Instead of acting like any normal tourist would have—which would be to alert everyone he had seen a wolf—he remained quiet, as if seeing a wolf in the wild was a day-to-day thing for him. He simply watched her.

Easing into the safety of the brush again, she took off at full run. Albert waited, well out of view of the other boat. She expected him to throw the wet pack at her, but instead, he waved her in.

"You might want to come to camp. Will radioed there has been coyote activity."

Shifting into human form took a second for her to let the discomfort pass before dealing with Albert's statement. "At the camp? But that would mean they had to cross the water." It also meant Will, the cook at the campsite, had been there alone.

"Or, they took their lazy asses up the road fifteen miles and crossed there then hoofed it in. That seems pretty desperate to me."

"Me, too."

The coyotes *were* desperate. Their band leader had given her an ultimatum—become his mate and merge their groups, or he would take her and her pack by force. But until now, only Jeb, the coyote Alpha, had shown any balls. The others still ran at the thought of being near the wolves.

"Will suggested, and I agree, you better get your

scent all over the camp. They're intimidated, if not scared of you, and if your scent has kept them out of the compound, maybe it will keep them off the camp."

Once they reached the banks of the site, Ripley helped unload the packs and coolers to the holding area along the path where the guests would later collect their things to take up the two-hundred yard path to the campsite. She immediately grabbed Zames' pack, opened it, removed the expensive black backpack, and rifled through his stuff.

"Who brings only new items when they're camping? Every item in this pack, from toothbrush to jeans, is brand new."

"Walt said he's in the area on business and decided to give us a try. Maybe he only had three-piece suits."

"I could believe that if at least his toiletries and underwear weren't also recently bought." Laying the contents of the bag on the bench, she searched the bottom.

"What exactly are you looking for?"

"I don't know, but it's not here, that's for sure." Placing everything as it had been, she returned the pack to its dry sack and set it with the others for the tourists to take with them to camp. "You want help with those coolers?"

"Nope, I got this. Besides, if you want to be gone by the time the raft gets here, you'd best get to it, boss lady."

With a wink, she headed into the woods, determined that every animal in the area would know she had been here.

**

Her scent saturated everything in the area from the fucking branches to his damned tent.

Throwing his backpack on one of the three wooden cots in the semi-permanent tent he'd taken as his for the night, Z leaned over as lustful urges he hadn't experienced in thirty-seven years wracked his body. His desire to drive his cock into Ripley Greystone was stronger than even the urges he'd had for his deceased mate, 21, or T, as everyone had called her. Hit by a car while on a mission, T had been unable to heal. Before he could reach her, she'd died. One of his own kind, she'd been a damned good Infiltrator.

They had been raised together, hunted, and trained. For a while, they'd even gone on missions as a couple, until the pack assigned them to work separately. For almost four decades since her death, Z'd been content to be alone and work on his own.

Now, after being dormant for so long, his libido roared to life in full, cockstand force. It didn't help everything he desired in a woman converged in Ripley—independent, physically fit, but not thin since she still had some meat on her bones, with hips that filled out jeans insanely well. But, more than anything, she was natural, wearing no makeup, the splatter of freckles across her nose giving her an appearance of innocence.

She had been here recently, within hours in fact, and Z would bet the grey wolf he had seen on the riverbank and Ripley were one and the same. She'd been downwind from him, so he hadn't been able to determine everything he wanted, but the hackles on his neck rose and his wolf screamed to claim her—his mate.

What she experienced he didn't know. Having hid his scent, he had no idea what that would do to her natural instinct to connect with one's mate. For certain, he had smelled her arousal the moment it hit her, and, as a result, he hadn't been able to read a single word on the waiver they had given him.

Now, he had a choice. He could finish his

assignment and leave with her none the wiser, or he could follow the desire every nerve ending in his body demanded—claim her and fuck her until she submitted to him. Unfortunately, at the moment, he had to play human for a while longer. Z still had to figure out the goings-on with her pack. Although he hadn't perceived anything malicious from any of the Greystones, he had yet to meet their Alpha and Enforcer, both of whom would be a gauge for why Ripley had made the trek out to beg Drew for protection, if indeed either their Alpha or Enforcer were aware Ripley had gone at all.

Leaving his tent, Z headed along a well-worn dirt path, past the other tents and his fellow campers. He declined the beer they offered but promised to join them later, which he had no plans to do. Moving along, he continued until reaching the open-air mess tent, where Will, the cook, busied himself grilling steaks.

The young blond man screamed omega. "Dinner will be ready in about half an hour. Feel free to munch on some salsa, start the campfire if you want, or grab a chair."

"Thanks. Whatever you're making smells awesome."

"Wait until you taste it. We pride ourselves on the juiciest, most tender steaks." Will repositioned the foil-wrapped meat around the grill. "After all, if the food isn't tasty as well as nourishing, what's the purpose of cooking it?"

"I have a friend who could take some classes from you." Scooping some salsa, Z popped it in his mouth. He closed his eyes as flavor erupted through his taste buds. If the Omega could make salsa nearly an orgasmic experience, what the hell could he do with steak and beans? "Do you stay out at camp all the time?"

"Pretty much. During the summer I'm here six out of seven days. I would stay all the time, even off-season, if Ripley didn't think I had to go back to town once a week."

"So, even when there are no overnighters, you stay?"

Will lifted the cover to check the beans in a cast iron pot. "Yep, sure do. Someone is always on the property for several reasons. One, we don't want squatters coming in and staying. And then there are wild animals. When I'm not around, someone else has to stay."

"Even in the off-season?"

"Nah. The tents all have to come down, and this culinary piece of heaven dismantled for the winter, all to be rebuilt at the first thaw of spring. This is a good gig if you can get it."

"How long have you been with Grey Wolf River Rafting?"

"About two seasons."

A lie. The river guide, Eric, had given the exact same answer and, although their hair color and styles had changed, and Will now wore a full beard, the site group photo from four years earlier contained the same people. The Internet made being paranormal a bit harder, as the lifespan of most shifters was three times that of a human. Hiding that fact and the slow aging process could be difficult.

"Sounds like the perfect job."

"Can't think of any place I would rather be." Will smiled, and despite his reservations, Z found the joy in the younger male contagious.

The pack treated their omegas well. So many didn't, and Z found it refreshing. The three omegas he'd met had been happy, talkative, and good at what they did. They were physically strong, not run-of-the mill omegas, but any shifter worth his teeth could discern an omega easily. Even those at the camp who looked like dominants still had the air of being submissive. But all the woman were strong betas, the strongest he'd seen.

Z spun when a branch snapped on the trail leading to the river. Less than a second later, his cock came to full attention. Every fiber of his being knew who approached.

"Ripley, what are you doing here?" Will asked, genuine pleasure written on his face.

She'd pulled her hair into a ponytail and wore cargo shorts, hiking boots, and a tank top that didn't quite cover her ample breasts. Some men may prefer black-lace teddies. Not Z. With a beautiful woman in that ensemble, he would be putty in her paws.

"Hey, Will. I'm taking over for Eric. Gemma's showing signs of pre-labor, and she wanted her husband there. So, here I am."

"Rock on. I'll go let Eric know he is about to be a daddy and to get his hide to his wife's side," Will said before turning to Z with an impressed look. "You lucked out. No one knows this river better than Ripley. Hell, I don't think there's a guide out there who is better at rafting than her."

"Really." It seemed odd there had been no mention of Ripley listed on the website if her talents were so amazing. Will hiked toward the tents set on the hill away from the rest of the guests. Z looked at

Ripley. "How long have you been rafting?"

"All my life. I think I navigated this river before I could crawl." The love of the water burned on her face and in her blue eyes.

Reaching for the bowl of chips, he grabbed one, staying nonchalant, when all he wanted to do was mark her as his. Something that proved more difficult the longer they were together. "So is this the only river you run?"

"For a while it has been, but in my twenties I rafted the Colorado and the Snake. Spent a season on the Salmon. But this one calls to me."

Typical of many packs, when wolves went through puberty, they were sent out on their own to find themselves and hone their skills. Usually the dominant males left, but sometimes strong betas, too.

"So, having spread your wings, you came home."

"This is where my family is." The electric zap caused by her smile nearly brought him to his knees. "So, what brings you to our rafting company?"

"A friend suggested it," Z said.

She was obviously hunting for answers of her own, trying to drag any info from him she could. Not that he'd make it easy for her.

He added, "I was coming this way for work when I

realized I was in the area and thought, what the heck. My friend has been trying to get me to take a five-day rafting trip, but I figured I should try a day-trip first. Fortunately, the town nearby had all the gear I could hope to buy. Somehow, I figured three-piece suits didn't seem the right attire."

Her shoulders eased at his answer, her walls coming down, if only a bit. "Smart move taking a short trip. Nothing worse than getting an hour out on a multi-day tour and finding out you hate it."

"That happen often?" He hoped the more he chatted with her, the more details he could gain about the pack and whatever problems they were having. He had ruled out an abusive Alpha. The omegas were treated well, and they'd be first in line as punching bags for sick, power-hungry wolves. And the betas, with the exception of Ripley, were full of smiles and cheer. She, on the other hand, appeared guarded and always on alert.

"Not too often, but more than you would think." She turned to Will as he came around the grill. "How long till the grub's ready?"

He sniffed the air—nothing a human would have noticed. "About twenty. Enough time to check those tracks I found on the hill."

"My thought exactly, Will."

"Animal tracks? Mind if I join you?" Z asked. The tall hill would give him a vantage point to see the area better, and with her by his side, he might also glean some information from her.

"Not at all."

But she did mind, her jaw muscles tightening on a smile. However, she wouldn't stop a paying customer from exploring the grounds.

Heading toward the steep hill behind the mess tent, she said, "Know much about animal tracking?"

As the two of them hiked the hill, with Ripley in front, her ass at eye level, Z's cock pointed straight up. He forced his focus back to what she had asked him. "My dad taught me how to track coyotes on our land as a boy."

She stumbled and fell forward, and he grabbed her waist.

"Hey, are you okay"

She leaned against his front and had to be aware of his erection. She remained motionless for a moment, and Z couldn't move, fearing this would be the only time he would have her so close. Her warmth rushed through his blood. How had he forgotten this closeness with a woman? Oh right...because thinking of a life with it had been too much to bear after T's death.

Five minutes or thirty seconds passed, he had no clue, but Ripley finally stepped away and continued up the hill.

"We're having issues with coyotes. Maybe you can be of help."

Though she sounded like nothing had happened, her voice took on a breathiness that had nothing to do with overexertion, though Z figured she hoped he would believe that. At the top of the hill, he immediately spotted evidence of coyotes, their paw prints clear in the dried mud. Kneeling, he traced the impressions the pads made.

"How much rain have you gotten this week?"

"Enough to saturate."

He would have preferred to be in wolf form for this investigation, but that would have to wait until after dark as everyone slept. Hopes for a night of uninterrupted rest dashed away like dust in the wind. "Enough to wash away any other evidence?"

"No, just a consistent sprinkle. Why?"

"See these here? There are several paw prints. These," he gestured toward several close together, " belong to one coyote. You see how the impression is deeper? But these belong to two others. This one's fourth pad is bent at a bizarre angle like it has something lodged in its paw, or the animal had been hurt and it didn't heal right."

"Okay, so you think we're dealing with at least three?"

As she searched around for more prints, he raised his nose to smell the air, but her scent overwhelmed him to the point of eliminating all others. "They spent a great deal of time here. Yet there is no scat."

She opened her mouth then rotated away from him. "Maybe we're missing it."

T- Rex would have left a lesser trail. No, it meant these weren't coyote animals, but coyote shifters, and Z would bet his sizable bank account the issues her pack dealt with revolved around this event. He still had more questions than answers, but at least at this point the Greystone Pack posed no threat to the Taos. Standing, he hadn't been aware she was in the process of returning to reinvestigate the paw prints until too late.

A hairsbreadth divided them, and it took all the willpower he processed to fight the building desire to pull her into his arms. Her breathing quickened, and as he gazed into her blue eyes, her raw sensuality forced him deeper into the cavernous pit he'd fallen in when he'd first seen her.

The words came out on a whisper. "You feel it, too, don't you?"

"This attraction?" Z raised an eyebrow.

She closed her eyes. "It won't work. I have secrets you could never understand."

"We all have secrets," he said then gave in to his animal nature and claimed her lips, though touching her nowhere else. He burned himself into her, forcing her to recant her words of denial.

It will work. He didn't know how, but he didn't think he could walk away from these feelings again. Having ensured the Greystones posed no threat to the Tao Pack, he could make his top priority the safety of his mate. His second would be to figure out the logistics of having a mate not of his pack.

Her deep groan rumbled through him, and every thought but Ripley faded. Passion swirled and something new, something different...something more, accompanied by a fizz running along his spine and through his nervous system, charging his powers. The urge to howl grew.

The dinner bell rang, forcing him to break the kiss. They stared at each other for a minute before she brought trembling fingers to her lips. As she twisted away, he gripped her arm.

"Before we head back, tell me how aggressive the coyotes are in this area."

She took a deep breath to center herself. "They're getting more so. But they aren't native here, and the nearest crossing for them is a good ten miles downriver." She rubbed her hips. "So, from where they usually prowl, it's a good fifteen miles."

"You said the river crossing?"

Ripley pointed in the general direction of what he assumed would be the crossing point. "Yeah, like I said, it's downriver from here. It's the only place to cross for about forty miles."

"Yes, but they can swim."

She looked at him, shocked. "That's not possible."

"They're very good swimmers, actually."

"My father always told us they hated water. That's why we put this camp here." The fear on her face replaced any remnants of sensuality. "Crap on a cracker!"

There were far stronger words he would have personally used. But then perhaps she was used to toning it down when children could be within earshot. "If they were to swim across, how close would they be?"

"Taking in that nothing could swim through some sections because of the eddies?"

"What the hell is an eddy?"

"Basically, where the water churns. There are some deadly ones in this area. It's why you need permits to boat the Wolf River."

Z understood her disbelief. If her Alpha had told her they were safe, she would have believed him. Unfortunately, the safety had been an illusion. Now to get all the information he could in order to best figure out how far the coyote band resided. Because this wasn't simply three lone dogs. There were more waiting somewhere. The tracks he and Ripley had spotted had been left behind by scouts.

"Okay, so taking into account a safe place to swim across, how far are they?" Z asked again.

She turned back toward the river. "Too close. Less than three miles."

Much nearer than he preferred. And why would her father let his pack believe coyotes couldn't swim? That left them and their tourist guests dangerously unprotected and with a false sense of security. These coyotes were after something and getting braver, by the little evidence he could collect.

Z, never one to sugarcoat anything, not with his mate's safety at stake, said, "Will is out here alone. Does he have a means of protecting himself?"

"He has a gun."

A wolf with a gun didn't ease Z's concerns any. "Would he use it?"

Her shoulders dropped in defeat. "No."

"You can't leave him here by himself. When we leave tomorrow, he should, too."

"Who are you?" She sniffed the air.

Ignoring her, Z asked, "Tomorrow, will you go somewhere private so we can talk? I will tell you anything you want to know." He cupped her face. How he wanted to allow his scent to come back to the surface, to remove the spell he'd cast to hide it from everyone. But he couldn't, not yet. Her emotions would overwhelm her once she sensed him. And if her arousal pheromones were any stronger, he wouldn't be able to stop either of them from claiming each other. "But tonight, you must trust me. Can you do that?"

She nodded, stepping away before descending the hill. "I shouldn't trust you. Nothing about you adds up. But, like our connection, I know I have to trust in you."

Obviously, she still believed him human, but she needed time to sort out what she felt. Once Ripley had the facts, all the pieces would fall into the place, forcing her to see they were mates. Her reaction to that was anyone's guess, but Z wouldn't force her when there were a dozen humans and a member of her pack around. He would give her space tonight, and that would allow him the time necessary to scout out on the area. Yet knowing she slept in a tent mere yards away might prove the hardest thing he'd ever ignored.

Chapter Three

Sometimes having something to keep the mind busy was the only thing that kept a person sane. And Ripley felt anything but sane the next morning. Zames's kiss had left her unsure her knees would hold as she'd worked her way back to camp the night before. For the remainder of the evening, he had maintained his distance, but his eyes were always on her, burning into her, devouring her.

After breakfast he caught her alone, reminding her of their agreement before he'd kissed her like something out of a chick flick. Zames also supported her when she informed Will she wanted him back at the compound.

"Ripley, that's stupid. I'll be fine out here."

"Don't argue." Ripley never raised her voice to her omegas but had to make him understand she would accept no argument. His safety and that of any members in her protection was of utmost importance. If she thought merging with the coyotes would be the right thing to do, and they would have created a better, safer life, she'd put aside her pride and do it. But the coyotes were the worst thing that could happen to them and Jeb, their leader, the worst of Alphas, cruel and selfish.

"Please, Will, don't make me worry. I want you in that boat and heading out of here when we leave."

"Yes, boss," he agreed, his voice tinged with a snark. Anyone could tell he didn't agree with her directive.

After breakfast, she navigated the river. She and the water acted as a team—one traveling, the other determining the direction. Those in the boats paddled. She didn't want them near the pitfall of fallen trees and shallow rocks that could get them hurt. And staying busy would at least allow her not to think about that damned kiss. Well, either of the kisses.

"Forward...that's it," Ripley shouted, the commands rolling off her tongue second nature.

In the front of the boat, paddle in hand, Zames took charge, and they all paddled together. What Ripley wouldn't give for him to have the shifter gene; for them to be true mates and for him to take on her pack. They needed an Alpha, and if Drew Tao wasn't interested, they would broaden their search. But Zames couldn't be the answer to their prayers. A human, no matter how Alpha-male, still could never be

Alpha enough to hold the coyotes at bay much longer.

"All stop," she yelled, slowing the boat.

It would get rough from there on. The rain lately hadn't been enough to raise the river. The rapids, usually low class III, had become class IV due to the rocks being closer to the surface. Ripley could negotiate them with no problem, but to do so the passengers had to work with her. listen to her commands, and use their paddles only as she deemed necessary. To ensure they all came through while remaining in the boat, their paddling had to work in tandem with her oars.

"I want everyone to paddle hard for the next three rapids."

"Remember, follow the person in front of you," Zames said with an authority no one in the boat dared to argue.

He herded the smaller children closer into the middle, telling one to hold onto him if she got scared, all the while double-checking their life vests. These were not the actions of a man who pled ignorance about adventure, even if his knowledge of rafting amounted to very little.

Ripley added, "And if by some fluke anyone gets thrown out, remember to point your feet toward the sky and downstream. I promise you will stay with the boat."

"Have you ever had anyone fall out?" one of the mothers asked.

"Not in a very long time." Ripley smiled, unable to count how many years had passed since she had thrown someone from the boat. "You'll be fine. Wedge that foot into the side of the raft if you want a little more leverage. Double-check that your life jackets are snug."

"I can barely breathe as it is," another woman complained.

"Good, then it's perfect," Ripley said with a wink.

The other rafts were in sight, so she turned hers around and took the rapid. Her heart pumped, and she breathed in the aromas around her. The crisp air, the fresh water, the fear and excitement coming off the humans. Gripping her oars, she maneuvered the boat to the top.

"All forward."

The raft lurched and away they went, and she became one with the vehicle, guiding it and its passengers through the gauntlet until they returned once again to the calm waters on the other side, a little wetter, but all in one piece and still in the boat.

The river, having vented her displeasure, welcomed once again. This was why Ripley loved it; it gave as much as it took, as peaceful as it was violent and, in the end, ever-changing because the water passing them would never be quite the same again.

The passengers cheered, exiting the rapids. Ripley reached the water's edge and spun the boat so they could best watch the other two. She had faith in her handpicked guides since she'd trained every one. Both boats came through with few problems. In the summer, they ran the route sometimes three times a day, depending on demand.

Thirty minutes later, she pulled the raft up to the unloading dock.

Tessa, another one of her betas who drove the bus, met them. "How's the river? Did she play nice?"

"As nice as she ever does." Ripley couldn't deny she felt better than she had in weeks, perhaps months. Being out on the water renewed her sense of life and hope.

"Did Will make it to headquarters?" Zames asked, assisting her in moving the boats onto the concrete dock.

"You speak like a soldier, do you know that?" Ripley nudged him then ripped off her life vest.

Tessa pulled the last and smallest boat out of the water with ease. "Will hadn't arrived when I left the office."

"When did you leave?" Ripley tried to wish away the panic rising within her.

"About forty minutes ago."

"He should have arrived by then. Something's wrong," Ripley said.

"Leave the raft," Zames demanded. "Leave the fucking raft, now. Take us to where we can cross again."

Fear engulfed her. Zames hadn't raised his voice or cursed in the twenty-four hours since he'd walked into her life. And yet, even in that short time, she knew it wasn't in his nature and meant they needed to act without delay.

"What do you think?" she asked.

"I think he's in trouble. Now, get everyone on the bus as quickly as possible without raising an alarm. Can you call your Alpha and get him to send someone? Your Enforcer or a few dominants over to check it out before we get there?" =

Stopping in her tracks, she turned on him. "What did you say?"

"Get some help," he said without pause.

"No, you didn't say help. You know about my people?" Her voice dropped in tone on the last word. *What the hell did this human know?*

"I do, but now isn't the time. Will—"

Keeping her voice low so no one else could hear proved hard when all she wanted to do was scream at this man. "I am not letting you near another member of my pack until—"

He cupped her face. "Listen to me very carefully. I am not the enemy, I will never hurt you. I can't. I promise to tell you everything after we deal with Will. Right now, you need to get your Enforcer over to the camp immediately."

"We're closer. We keep a boat hidden not too far from the campsite. We can use it to cross and see if Will is still there." Zames was right. They needed to focus on Will and his safety first. Something told her she could trust Zames and that scared the hell out of her.

Ripley faced her guides. "Can you two get these ready for the second tour?"

"Of course. What's wrong?" Anne, the eldest of her guides, asked.

"I don't know yet, but hopefully nothing."

"Ripley, who the hell is that guy?" Though Anne

voiced it, Ripley judged by their upraised eyebrows, Tessa and the Babs had the same question.

"He's...a friend."

Bab's lips twitched "Friend, huh? I would love a *friend* like him."

As much as Ripley would enjoy bantering with the horny trio, her only concern at the moment was Will. After getting the correct head count, she boarded the bus, sitting right behind the driver. Zames slid in beside her, his heat warming the cold chill running through her.

"I should have made sure he left."

"He's a grown man who'd told you he would leave minutes after us."

Ripley gave into the urge and leaned toward Zames. He kissed the top of her head before wrapping a reassuring arm around her.

"Can you drive the bus back for us, so Tessa and I can check on Will?" she asked.

"I'm not leaving your side."

Turning in order to see him better, she shook her head. "I can't let you do that."

"Whatever secrets you're afraid I will discover, stop worrying. We'll deal with them later, but right now we have to focus."

The ten minutes it took to get to the boat seemed closer to ten hours. Neither she nor Zames bothered with life vests. As they came within view of the camp landing, the motorboat Will would need to use to get out of camp sat there as a bad omen, and coolers lay open on the sandy ground nearby. Zames jumped out, yanking the boat in and putting a finger to his lips. The trail to the camp showed no signs of life. That alone told her what she dreaded.

He moved ahead of Ripley with the stealth precision of a Navy SEAL. If only he were wolf, he would make a perfect mate, perhaps even an Alpha.

Her skin crawled at the high-pitched shouts and woots of men in the distance. As she and Zames rounded the bend, the coyotes came into view. One of them kicked something, or *someone*, near the campfire.

"Stop it," she yelled, unable to stay put as they attacked what had to be Will. Running into the open, she paused. Five of the coyote-clan baddies stared back at her.

"You got here quicker than expected, Miss Ripley," one the men said, thankfully downwind from her because she could almost see the stink coming off him.

As two of them stepped toward her, Zames pushed

her behind him, making sure he stood between her and them. "You take one step closer to my mate, and I will tear each of you limb from limb."

Mate? Did he say mate?

The largest of the group stepped forward, sniffed the air, and laughed. "What do you plan to do, human? Call 911?"

One second, the handsome human protector stood before her, and a blink of an eye later, a large black wolf replaced him, growling, its teeth bared. It happened so fast Ripley still searched for Zames beside her. *Impossible.* No wolf shifted *that* quickly or easily. The world around her spun, and her stomach lurched.

The coyotes had taken a few steps forward then just as quickly turned tail and ran.

Movement from the corner of her eye brought Ripley back to reality. But before she could get to Will, the black wolf had resumed human form and knelt beside him.

"Get some water and rags, quickly," he growled.

"Zames, I don't understand...."

"Z. My name is Z, and I promise I'll tell you everything. But I need the water now."

She ran to the mess tent a few feet from them. Pulling the ten-gallon water containers out, thankful

Will had listened and not dumped them, she rested one on her shoulder. The towels were harder to find, but she located some stacked behind the pots and pans. As she'd approached Z, he'd returned to wolf form and retrieved sleeping bags from the nearest tent. She hadn't been aware he'd left Will's side. His focus remained on Will as he tucked the bags around the injured omega.

"He's in shock. We have to get him warm. Is there a phone or radio you can use to call for help?"

"We have to get him to our healer." Wiping clammy palms on her shorts, Ripley tried to concentrate. Her brain swirled, desperate to make heads, or in this case, black wolf tails of what had happened.

Without taking his eyes off Will, Z wrapped another sleeping bag around his still body. "Your Alpha should get his ass out here and deal with this."

She grabbed the satellite phone they used for emergencies hanging from one of the mess tent poles. Ripley's youngest sister, Jordan, answered but Ripley didn't wait for pleasantries.

"Send Janey out to the campsite now. "

"She's laboring with Gemma."

Z snatched the phone from Ripley. "Tell Janey

61

unless Gemma is near to delivery, it is a matter of life or death for Will at the moment. The sooner she gets here, the better."

He threw the phone down and attended to Will, whose moans had grown softer. After disconnecting the cell, she knelt beside the omega. Taking the wet cloths, she cleaned his face to better assess the damage. Z chanted something low, and although she had keen hearing, she couldn't understand the words. But as they passed his lips, Will calmed until he seemed to fall into a restful sleep.

Z stood, reaching for her. "He will rest until Janey gets here. There is nothing more we can do now."

"I don't want to leave him."

"We aren't going far. Just out of his hearing. You have questions, but I have answers only you can hear."

She placed her hand in his and followed him to the benches a few feet away. "Who are you?"

"Your mate."

She pulled away then regretted the loss of his touch. "Yeah, I got that, but why are you here? And why can't I smell you?"

"My real name is Z, not Zames. Drew Tao sent me."

Unable to sit, she shot to her feet. Why the hell

would the Tao Alpha send someone when he'd made it clear he could not help them? "Why?"

"He needed information you were unable or unwilling to give him."

"What do you do for the Taos?"

"I'm not part of their pack, but I do help Drew out when I can. I'm an Infiltrator."

"Infiltrator." A moment ago, Ripley couldn't sit still, but now her feet felt frozen in the dirt. "You mean the creatures that shifter mommies and daddies tell their children will sneak in, in the middle of night, and get them if they don't behave? Monsters of legend?"

"We aren't monsters, but we do sneak. Think of us more along the line of the James Bonds of shifters."

"So, what...you were sent to spy on us?" Of all the jackhole-ish things she had dealt with, having someone send a spy into their midst ranked as one of the worst.

"Drew had concerns."

Her laugh came off as angry as she felt. "Why? He took all of five minutes to decide he didn't want to help us then threw us to the coyotes."

"Ripley." Z reached out as if to soothe her.

"Don't. Just don't." If he touched her, the anger she felt would fade away with the hormonal urges she couldn't control.

"Drew had no choice. You weren't helping him. He needed more information."

"So, when I wouldn't give it freely, he decided to send his pit bull out to find it."

"The Tao Pack has been through hell in the last half-century, but you wouldn't know because *your* pack hid from everyone. For all Drew knew, your Alpha sent you to sniff out the weaknesses still left in it."

Ripley stepped back at the mention of her Alpha, and judging by Z's raised eyebrow, he'd noticed. She doubted there was much he didn't catch

"So, tell me, Ripley, where the hell is the Greystone Alpha? Your Enforcer? Hell, how about a male who isn't an omega?"

"I think I hear the boat." She hoped she heard it, anything to distract Z from asking more questions she couldn't answer.

He grabbed her arm, twisting her around to look at him. "Say what I already know. Confirm what I suspect."

"I can't. Not even to you."

"Do you trust me?"

Shaking her head, she tried to jerk out his grasp,

but he was far stronger than her. "I don't know you."

"Your soul does." He closed his eyes and exhaled, and all of a sudden his scent surrounded her, engulfed and overrode her senses. She growled deep, the answering urge to cover him with her scent overwhelming her. It screamed to her wolf, calling for them to be one. "You accept you are my mate."

She nodded, her knees weakening. "I can't change the Fates."

"Perhaps what you don't understand is I can't harm you or allow any harm to come to you. As my mate, you are in my protection whether you accept me or not."

She searched his eyes to determine whether he lied, but found only truth.

When he next spoke, his tone softened. "Tell me."

On a stuttering breath, she closed her eyes to give voice to words she had never spoken. "There is no Alpha, not anymore. No dominant males, and no Enforcer either, and there haven't been since before I was born."

"The last Alpha?"

"My father died twenty years ago when I was twenty-three. I have been charged with keeping the pack safe. We've been holding off the coyotes ever since."

She hadn't known what to expect, but Z pulling her into his arms hadn't been it. "I am so sorry."

Sorry? What the hell did he have to be sorry about? "What? Why?"

"For so long, since my wife died, I have blocked myself off from feeling anything. She wasn't my true mate, everyone knew that, but I loved her. And because I.... I didn't think there might be someone out there who wanted me." He pulled back enough to place a kiss on Ripley's lips. "I betrayed you by not opening myself to the understanding that the universe had someone else."

Into his chest, she spoke. "What we need is an Alpha, and you would—"

"I can't."

"What do you mean, you can't? You're strong enough." She tried to step away, but he held strong.

"I am forbidden from taking on Alpha of any pack—" When she shoved against him in anger, Z said, "Wait a second, calm yourself. I'm going to ask Drew to take your pack under his wing. He can be your Alpha."

"We didn't want him as our Alpha. We just wanted some protection from Jeb and his dogs."

"Jeb?"

"The coyote's Alpha, if you can call him that." Ripley wanted some space, but the draw to touch Z was too strong.

"What's wrong with Drew?"

"The reason our pack went stealth so many years ago was because of Drew's father, Magnum Tao. Magnum was mentally unstable. My father knew we were in trouble and that the Taos were ruthless. He feared for his daughters' safety."

"Drew isn't his father."

"What if his father passed his insanity to his son?"

"Then he will die by my hand or that of his Enforcer's. He made us promise." Lifting her chin so she would meet his eyes, Z added, "He is a good man. Do you think I would leave the protection of my mate to just any wolf?"

Ripley felt he would have said more, but the scuffling behind them of someone approaching interrupted the conversation. Will required their attention. They had gone this long without an Alpha, waiting a few more hours or days wouldn't hurt. Besides, they had a dominant wolf in the pack, at least for the time being, and the coyotes had already discovered Z's presence.

Chapter Four

Z's sister answered the phone. "What's wrong?"

"Why would anything be wrong, N?"

"Because you text occasionally but never call."

And now for the hard part—how to get what he required without answering the question of his pack's best interrogator and information keeper. "Are the twins still under pack arrest?"

"Yes, the damned council doesn't realize taking them off jobs and making them stay here is punishing those of us who choose to stay packside."

"I have to have them here helping me. Can you make that happen? Like 'get them here in the next four hours' happen?"

"You? You want them?"

Z had expected her incredulous response. He never asked for help or worked with anyone. Not since T had died.

N sighed. "Okay, what gives, and I'll know if you're lying. This has to do with the Greystone Pack, right?"

"Yes." He watched the now-empty parking lot at the Greystone Wolf River Rafting Tours building from the wooden deck that came off the side of the building. Ripley had gone into the office to make sure all the tours happening later in the week were set. They didn't have another overnight for a few days, which would give Z an opportunity to add protections to the campsite. He'd taken the downtime to call in the reinforcements. "The pack hasn't had an Alpha in decades and is being stalked by a foul band of coyotes."

"Is there any other kind of coyote?" N asked, her disgust apparent even over the phone.

His sister, more than most of his kind, hated coyotes. She had been attacked by a group of coyote scouts while on one of her first missions. Z had arrived in time to save her life, but he'd never known how much damage had truly been done. When he'd finished with the dogs, he couldn't tell their blood from hers. After that, N never returned to the field, but chose to work from within the safety of the pack.

"Not to my knowledge, but regardless, the pack has to have protection," Z said.

"Z, did you bestow information without my having to pull teeth to get it?"

And the sister he so loved, the one who would nag and nag until she dragged every ounce of information she could out of him, sounded stunned. If the situation didn't require immediate attention, he might have basked in the moment.

"I don't have time for this. Can you get the twins here or not? This pack is in serious trouble."

"So, why not take them to another local pack, like, I don't know, the Taos?"

Frustrated, Z growled. "Do you want me to get the twins out of your hair or not?"

"Yes, but you can't blame me for being curious about my big brother. Because with everything you're freely sharing, there's something you aren't telling me." She wouldn't let this go, she would text and call and eventually come out herself to badger him until he caved.

Taking a deep breath, he braced himself. "The pack leader is my mate. Her name is Ripley, and I will tell you more later. Right now, you have to send our baby brothers on a plane heading in my direction."

"Wait, you can't—"

Ending the call, Z stood outside and watched Ripley through the window as she stirred about her office. She appeared unsure of herself, fidgeting with a pencil one minute then shifting from one foot to the other the next. He couldn't blame her. Unlike her, he had once loved and subsequently felt nothing but numb for decades. He thanked the Fates for the emotions coursing through him now, waking him.

Taking a few steps, he closed his eyes and opened his senses to everything around him, making sure no one was about. Then he entered the building to find Ripley bent over her desk. His mouth went dry imagining what he could do to her on that flat surface.

To divert his attention, he stepped over to the coffee pot and poured a cup. "My twin brothers will be here by nightfall. One will stay and help patrol the pack's safety, and the other will stay out with whomever is at the campground."

She huffed. "Taking right over, I see."

"Where your safety and that of your family is concerned, you're damned straight. You don't have to accept what fate lays before us, and I certainly won't force you, but where your safety is concerned, I won't negotiate. And you don't have any other options than to accept the help I'm giving at the moment."

Her shoulders dropped in defeat. "That was uncalled for. I'm sorry. I'm still so angry about Will, and I feel guilty. Then there is the swirl of emotions around you. I have no idea how to deal with you."

Placing a cup of coffee before her, he leaned against the wall. "It's been a hell of a twenty-four hours for you."

"I don't feel as if there is an end in sight to this hell."

He could simply lift her in his arms and take her somewhere safe. Maybe somewhere safe with a large bed and room service. Instead, he would do something he'd never done before—he'd be selfless.

"Do you want me to leave? Close enough that if you call, I can be here, but far enough you have some space?"

Her blue eyes burned into his soul. "No, I think closer."

His cock came to full attention. "How close?"

Eyes never leaving his, she removed first the flannel shirt she wore, letting it fall soundlessly to the floor. Then taking a few more steps toward him, she unbuttoned her jeans. His mouth salivated as she pushed the denim over her hips and thighs. He had no idea when her shoes came off, but she stood before him, sexier than Aphrodite, in a pair of white cotton panties, a tight men's white cotton tank top, and gray wool socks gathered around her ankles. He allowed her one more step before yanking her into his arms. His cock strained against the new black jeans he hadn't had a chance to break in yet. She pulled at his T-shirt, fighting the fabric to get it over his head. She was a woman determined, her only thought evidently getting him naked.

His thoughts exactly.

"Space is the last thing I want. I need you to fully claim me as your mate."

The words fizzed through him like a fuse on a stick of dynamite, the flame growing ever closer to its final destination. His mouth crashed over hers, claiming—branding. Her tank top, though thin, stood between them, hampering his progression. He fingered the neckline before effortlessly ripping it apart with both hands. Her full breasts bounced free, nipples alert.

Kicking off his shoes and getting rid of his jeans and underwear in one swift move, he lifted her by her ass until she rested against him. He loved the feel of her weight in his arms, the softness of her thighs wrapped around his waist, and her breasts pressing against his heart, which beat in perfect time with hers.

Walking them to the closest wall, he used it for leverage and thrust into her. He smelled her arousal, the musky scent driving his libido to new heights. As they became one for the first time, he finally understood so much he hadn't before—the importance of a true mate, the connection, and the amazing amount of power that raced through him as he claimed her.

She met every plunge with force, pushing her heels into his flanks to take him deeper. Her fingernails raked his back, drawing blood as her inner she-wolf came out. If she continued, he would never last.

"Give me your hands."

"Why?" She didn't argue though, nor did she fight him when he took her wrists and placed them above her head. Kissing her neck, he growled deep within his throat as she panted.

"Z...."

"What do you want?" He knew exactly what she wanted, but he had to hear her say the words.

"Please. Help me."

Vague didn't work for him, never had. So, he slowed his movements, drawing out each stroke until her pants turned into mewls. Her thighs clenched tighter, and she fought his grip holding her in place. "Please let me come."

"I live to fill your every desire." He captured her lips with his, and his tongue danced with hers. Increasing the speed, sensing by the tightening of her inner walls when she grew close, and when she finally flew, he allowed himself to join her, spilling his seed deep within her.

He released her, savoring the feel of her fingers when she worked them through his hair. He marveled at the spark evident in her eyes and the glow of her skin that had nothing to do with the sheen of sweat they both had.

"You are the most beautiful thing I have ever seen," he said between deep breaths.

"I never thought I would feel this, never thought I could find my mate." She palmed his face, focusing on his eyes. "Please be our Alpha."

"I can be yours, but not your pack's."

The front door of the office swung open, and Babs and Anne entered, having returned from their second rafting trip of the day. "Did you hear what he said about the rapid? If that jackass thought *that* was rough, he doesn't— Oh my God!"

Biting her lip, Ripley snuck a peek over Z's shoulder at her packmates and whispered, "Next time, we should lock the door."

"Perhaps that would be wise," he muttered. Having his ass bared to two of her guides wasn't a situation he'd ever expected to find himself in, but when his mate desired him, he could never refuse her.

Between gritted teeth, and never looking away from her, he demanded, "Do you two think you could step outside for a minute?"

"Oh, right. We'll head outside," one of them replied.

"That would be a fan-fucking-tastic idea."

As soon as the door clicked closed, he kissed Ripley hard before allowing her feet to touch the floor. After locating their clothes, they assisted one another in getting dressed again between caresses. Once he had his jeans zipped, he allowed the girls back into the office.

"You can chat with your boss now."

"We're really sorry. We had no idea you two were...well, you know."

"Yes, well it surprised to us, too." Ripley laughed while tying the laces of her boots. "Babs and Anna, meet Z, my mate."

"Mate? I thought you were human," Babs said, appearing gobsmacked

"That escalated fast," Anne said at the same time.

"Humans can mate with shifters." Z walked over to Ripley, placing an arm around her waist. "But I am a wolf."

"But I didn't smell...?" Anne started, but appeared

too confused to finish her thought.

Ripley said, "He stood downwind. You couldn't have smelled him. And I can attest he is majestic in wolf form."

"You are quite the she-wolf yourself." He rubbed his knuckles across her neck.

"I think I might vomit on all this sticky sweetness." Babs mimicked a gagging reflex.

Figuring a change in conversation would be appreciated, Z asked, "So, how is Will?"

"Janey has him resting comfortably," Anne answered.

Ripley stood, taking his hand in hers. "Let's go check on him, shall we?"

She was touching him to verify their connection. Some mates required constant connection, and as her mate, Z could do no less than give what she sought. He assumed since her pack lacked dominants, none of the betas would understand changes could happen during and after mating, or what to expect. And worse, he'd realized too late he'd be bringing two single and usually sex-crazed twins into the she-wolf's den. Z chuckled. He couldn't wait to see the boys getting eaten alive.

From her fingers to her toes, Ripley's body still sizzled. Every time the sensation became too strong, almost too much for her to bear, Z would reach for her, brush his lips against an area of exposed skin. He comprehended what she required even before she did. On the ride to the compound, he had filled her in on his pack and the rules that governed him and his own, and also about the two wolves about to descend on hers.

She couldn't say she completely understood, but at least she knew why he couldn't be Alpha, not *wouldn't* be Alpha. The oath he had taken years earlier still bound him, preventing his acceptance of the position or interfering in others' ability to hold the position. Knowing this didn't make Ripley happy, but she couldn't do anything to convince him to change his mind. Not that she wouldn't try.

So, some areas made more sense, but she still didn't quite get the naming thing they had—symbols, letters, and numbers.

"Is this desire to touch you normal?" she asked once they'd checked on Will and said hello to the newest member of the pack—the yet-unnamed omega boy baby who'd been born shortly after Janey returned with Will.

"Whatever you desire will be our normal. It doesn't matter what others do."

"So, it isn't normal?"

He shrugged. "What's normal really? I have observed more couples than I can count. Some, like you, have to touch their partners regularly, while others seemed to barely notice the other's presence. My pack doesn't hold out on finding their mate, but we usually find someone compatible to procreate with."

"You make it sound so passionless." She pulled away. "I'll try to be less clingy."

Z smiled, leaning into her. "It's fine. I can think of no one I would rather have cling to me. Simply because my people aren't full of public displays of affection doesn't mean you can't be. Be who you are, Ripley. It's why the Fates chose me for you."

"How will this work?" She wasn't sure what part of *this* she meant; there were so many things she didn't know would work. So, she figured he could pick and choose which *this* to answer.

"I can make this my home base, but I have to travel. The bad guys rarely come to me, more's the pity."

"So it's true," a deep male voice spoke from behind

them.

Someone else put in, "The solo Z has been done in by a mate."

Twisting, Ripley saw two men, exact replicas, standing before her. The same height as Z, their only difference being they were trimmer, where Z had a more muscular body. They also possessed a boyish and mischievous side Z lacked. They had a playfulness equal to her mate's seriousness

"Ripley, meet my baby brothers, D and Dumb."

"Not dumb, asshole." The one on the right put his hand out to greet her. "I'm 7, but everyone other than Zackhole here calls me Sev."

Zackhole? She found it hard to believe these two were related to Z. "It's a pleasure to meet you both."

The brothers circled around her. "Everyone is curious about you."

"N can't keep her mouth shut, can she?" Z asked, but he hadn't directed the comment to anyone in particular.

Besides, Ripley was too busy trying to keep focus with the way they circled her.

Shifting his attention finally, D assessed the common area of the small compound, taking in the communal kitchen, dining hall, and four housing buildings. "Did you imagine she could?"

The twins stopped short and sniffed the air. In a low voice, Sev asked, "What direction is the coyote band?"

Ripley pointed to the southwest corner of the property, and they shifted into black wolves as quickly as Z had, running full-out in the opposite direction of where she had pointed. Though large, their size couldn't compare to that of Z's, but they had an agility she hadn't seen in any wolf before. A minute later, a yelp reached the camp, followed by the black wolves dragging a struggling person behind them.

"They might be obnoxious, but I wouldn't trust anyone else to protect you," Z said.

Both wolves shifted back so fast the coyote didn't have a chance to move before he was within their grasp again.

"We aren't your guard dogs, Z." Sev growled.

"You want to return to fulfilling the term of the council's punishment? What is it...reorganizing all of their records?"

"Just call me Rover," D grunted, pushing the intruder toward Z's feet.

"There are three more out there. Want us to get them?" Sev asked, sniffing the air again.

"No, they've been watching us since we arrived. But I waited for you two to get here. I want them to see us and bring the news back to their bastard Alpha that there are dominants in this pack again."

"You knew they were there?" Ripley asked, trying to ignore the belligerent man struggling in vain to get away from the twins. "Z, there are children who play out here."

"I wouldn't be much of an Infiltrator if I hadn't sensed their presence. As for the children, they're all safely inside one of the housing units. The coyotes have to believe the betas are no longer alone. But, in case they don't get the message, I'm going to invite myself for a visit."

"Z, they have over thirty in their band."

"I only have to destroy one."

D came over and nudged her. "Z, she doesn't have much faith in your abilities."

"She hasn't known me but twenty-four hours. She hasn't seen my abilities yet."

She *had* seen some of his abilities. Well, maybe not seen so much as experienced, and those proved he could carry them both. She shook her head to throw out those thoughts.

D gave her a reassuring glance. "Really, they don't

stand a chance. They won't know he's there until it's too late."

"And even then, most won't know he ever came through at all," Sev added.

"It was a real pain in the ass when we were younger." D grimaced and rubbed his arm as if remembering a long gone, yet still painful childhood memory.

"You two interrogate this one and then deal with security issues on the perimeter. Take a beta or two with you to help." Extending his hand, Z pulled Ripley against him. "Where can we talk privately?"

"When you say private...?" she asked.

"Private, as in so no coyote ears can hear."

Her cheeks warmed since her brain and libido weren't thinking about *private chat*, but more like, *private, get naked*. "Gotcha. This way. The dining hall should be empty at this time of day."

"What were you thinking about that has put that delightful blush on your cheeks?" Z teased. She already doubted he allowed his playful side out much, if ever. He added, "To be honest, after a few decades of celibacy, a bedroom with you in it for a month sounds pretty damned awesome."

They took a seat at the end of the hall. Ripley bit

her lip, trying hard not to reach out for him. She had made it this long without a man but struggled with the unfamiliar desire to touch him all the time for reassurance. "You're going after them, aren't you?"

"There is no other way."

"But, I'm mated now. Jeb can't hurt—"

"He still wants this pack, and there are a ton of unmated women here. He'll keep coming. They're too stupid to do otherwise."

"Then I'm going with you."

"No."

Offended, anger rose within her. She expected this from some dominants but not from her mate. And not directed at her. "Why? Because I'm a woman?"

"No, because I work alone. I always work alone."

She stood. "That's stupid. I know where they live."

"I can follow their scent. They can't hide it. Believe me, one of your pups could find them."

"I'll follow you." Hands on her hips, she showed him the strong beta she'd always been. He may be her dominant, but that didn't mean she would become submissive overnight and bend to his every will. That wasn't part of her nature, nor how she'd been raised.

"Of course you will." He sighed and studied her. "Do you promise to do what I say? Not because you can't handle yourself, and not because I can't take orders from you. I took orders on the river just fine today, but this is what I do. And I can't fight those coming at me while I'm worried about you behind me."

"I promise." A compromise she could live with, and she didn't have to be in the thick of things. In fact, she hated fighting when she could prevent it, but she had to hunt beside him as his partner even if only as a guide, whether it be on the river or leading him to the enemy.

"Sounds like a party," D said, nearly causing her to jump out of her skin. The damned twins could show the Stealth Bomber a thing or two. "Can we play?"

"No."

"Come on, Z. You need us."

"I don't need you."

"Yes, you do, bro. Think about it; you can't say no to her." Sev chuckled as if enjoying his brother's discomfort. "We, on the other hand, do not suffer from your affliction. So you need us."

"To say no to her?"

"Not exactly." D took over where Sev left off. "If you're doing your thing, then she's left unprotected. Our job is to protect her while you can't, so you can focus."

In any other situation, Ripley would have been insulted, but her mate seemed so completely out of his comfort zone. "They have a point."

"Did she just agree with us?" D asked.

"I like her," Sev put in.

Frustrated, Z ran fingers through his hair and raised an eyebrow in Ripley's direction. "Please don't encourage them."

Leaning in, D whispered in her ear—at least she thought it was D, "No one ever agrees with us."

Before she could ask why, Z threw his hands in the air in defeat and headed toward the exit. "I'm done."

"He loves us."

"He doesn't know it yet."

She stared at the men, still unable to tell them apart, and for the first time in a very long while, she laughed, letting her troubles wash away.

Chapter Five

The ground sank beneath Z's paws, the rain from earlier in the week having left the land soft. Four wolves coming in undetected would be much harder to achieve and harder to hide. Before leaving the compound, he'd given his directives to the three amigos behind him to ensure they understood the rules. *His rules.* Ripley's safety first and foremost. He didn't want to take any chance of her being hurt. They were to stay far back, and were not to enter the coyote's lair. And Ripley, under no circumstances whatsoever, would enter the coyote camp. The twins were not to leave her side.

The moon reflected off her silvery-gray fur, another reason he didn't want her to come. Unlike all those in his pack whose fur camouflaged them in the dark, hers looked like spun silver.

The stench coming off the upcoming valley distracted him and forced him to pause. He wished he had the power of telepathy with his mate. But of his kind, only the twins had that talent. The closer the group got, the more questions he had. With his nostrils on fire from the potent stink, he wondered if perhaps the madness Magnum had suffered from hadn't also shown in the coyotes. They certainly didn't give a shit about their lair.

Ripley reached the designated stopping point and turned. Her concern shone in the deep-blue pools of her eyes. What she didn't know—couldn't know because they hadn't been together long enough for her to understand—was sneaking into the lair was cub's play. There were few as good as Z at what he did. If he thought for a minute this little mission of theirs would leave her alone again, he would have called in more help. The twins didn't count. The twins were good at protection and security, but recon...not so much.

Z brushed against her, nuzzling his muzzle into her thick, soft fur. Instead of blowing his scent away downwind so that no one would sense his presence as he usually would, he blew it on her, ensuring anyone who came close or made to take his mate would damned well know she belonged to him. Then he disappeared into the darkness. Quietly, stealthy, and undetectable to any of the idiots who thought to attack her family.

He entered their lair of derelict shacks, poor excuses for homes that littered the small area. A few had only tattered, old painter's tarps draped over the top of rickety, wood frames to keep the weather out. A bonfire lay on the east side of the camp. Five men and two women, unaware he stalked them, drank from one large clear-glass bottle. Over the stench, he couldn't make out what exactly they were partaking of but figured it was cheap wine or even cheaper moonshine. One of the men stood then fell dangerously close to the burning embers. It didn't matter—the seven were of no concern to him.

Ripley believed the coyote pack consisted of twenty-two males and a few females. Its lack of females drove them to the wolves, but Z had to find out why they weren't going for their own kind. In the end, the only thing he truly cared about was making sure the damned dogs stayed well away from her pack.

A drunk female stumbled out of the nicest of the shacks. She giggled before heading to the fire pit to join the others. Z closed his eyes and sent a push of his powers, finding the kinetic energy of one person in the shack. Entering the still-open screen door, he assessed the shabby, ill-kempt, lantern-lit room. It held very little—an old television, complete with a set of rabbit ears, a metal-frame bed with a bare, and very stained mattress. The smell coming off it alone nearly brought

Z's dinner back up.

Through the only other door, the Alpha entered with a thirty-two ounce beer in one hand and scratching his ass with the other. He wore nothing but tighty whities, which in the yellowish shape they were in, looked as bad as the bed smelled. The whole place made Z want to gag. The thought of this man, or any man there, touching Ripley or one of her sisters sent a rage through him and fired his blood, forcing his shift back to human form.

"What the fuck?" the coyote Alpha demanded, stumbling back in inebriated confusion.

Z wasted no time, using the moment of weakness to his advantage. Wrapping a hand around the skinnier man's neck, he rushed him against the peeling wall.

"You must be Jeb."

Unable to speak with Z's fingers around his larynx, the other man nodded, wide-eyed.

"I want you to listen and listen well. Ripley is mine."

The coyote tried to shift into his animal form, scratching at Z to let him go. Evidently, the cowards who had come to Ripley's camp that afternoon hadn't informed their Alpha of the small tidbit that dominants were in Greystone. In fact, Z hadn't seen the ones from earlier at all, leading him to believe they'd seen the writing on the wall and decided to take off on their own.

"You will cease your harassment of her and her pack."

"They...are...Alpha-less," the coyote rasped.

"Not anymore." Z hadn't actually gotten Drew to agree to that part yet, but Jeb could be kept in ignorance on that matter. "You'll take your band and get out. I want you gone before the full moon. I hear Yellowstone is a good place for coyotes right now."

Disbelief entered the other man's eyes. They both knew with the reintroduction of wolves to the park, Yellowstone was anything but safe for his kind. Not to mention, the bear shifters ruled sections of the park with iron paws.

Z didn't care as long as these coyotes put some distance between them. "Do I make myself clear?"

The coyote nodded, and Z released his grip, backing away to leave.

Jeb panted, glaring at him. "You have no right to tell me what to do with my band."

"Normally, I'd agree, but when you attack my mate's pack, I reserve the right to do anything to protect them. You're lucky I don't tear you limb from limb. But that worthless band out there doesn't have anyone capable of leading them, and I worry they'll show themselves to humans. For that reason only do I let you walk away with your life. But make no mistake, if I find you or yours sniffing around mine, I will tear your throat out."

Jeb started to shift, but unfortunately didn't know Z's speed or agility. Before Jeb's four limbs touched the ground to start his transformation, Z shifted into full wolf form and attacked.

The coyote squalled in agony as Z bit into his arm, dragging the Alpha from the shack and onto the dirt path pretending to be a road. Suddenly, the band surrounded Z. He bared his teeth, his hackles high, daring someone to show him an ounce of gumption. Not one member would give their life for their leader, or had the balls to step forward for the rest of their band.

A moment later, back in human form, he gave one more fierce kick to Jeb's side before hauling the man to his feet. "If any one of you ever come near the Greystones, or even sniff in the direction of my mate again, I will rip off your fucking heads. Understood?"

The coyotes, appearing conflicted between

stepping forward to defend their own or cowering in the corner of the camp, only nodded.

Jeb lowered his head, unable to make eye contacted with the dominant wolf, and announced in a muffled voice, "We are relocating."

"That is the first smart decision you have probably ever made for your pack." About to throw the man from him, Z spotted movement from the edge of the greenway. He should have been surprised to see Ripley coming through the forest's edge with twins as her bookends, yet he wasn't.

"We agreed you would let me deal with this," he said.

"She doesn't listen well," D mumbled

"It's quite annoying," 7 agreed.

Z would point out that the twins shared that same flaw at another time. "Ripley?"

"I wanted to watch the show." She growled at the coyote who stood in her way. When the animal yelped and ran, Z let the strange feeling of pride cover him. "I had no doubt you would take care of them."

He nodded. "Jeb here said they are about the leave the area."

Ripley smiled at Z, who still held the Alpha in a death grip, before approaching. "Jeb, you son of a bitch. You haven't the balls to attack me straight-on, so you attack my omega. You failed to realize our omegas are revered for their talents, not bullied and mistreated for their emotions."

Curling his upper lip in a snarl, he spat, "They are weak."

Ripley growled again, bared her teeth, and swung, hitting Jeb with enough force, the man went out like a light.

Z stumbled and dropped the unconscious coyote to the ground, making no effort to break his fall. After wiping his fists on his pants, he stepped over him then wrapped his arm around his mate. He took her hand in his. Looking over the reddened knuckles, he brought them to his lips to gently kiss. "Nice swing."

"Thanks. My dad taught me."

"Smart man. Are you ready to get out of here?" The question wasn't one he expected an answer to, and she must have sensed that since she followed his lead silently. He faced the coyote dominants, if one could call them that, sitting on the outer edge. When he took a step toward them, they lowered their heads.

"This band has one week, and not a day more, to have this land cleaned and be gone from it. Don't let me see or smell you here again."

The Alpha, regaining consciousness, stood on unsteady feet. "Where the hell are we supposed to go?"

"As I said before, try Yellowstone."

The Yellowstone wolf pack would garner no bullshit from these dogs. Its members were strong but fair. The bears were another issue, but not Z's to worry about.

Walking over, he grabbed Jeb by his collar and lowered his voice so only the other man could hear. "If I ever hear you're terrorizing another pack, I will hunt you to ground, and not even your worst nightmare can compare to what I will do to you. I am the Infiltrator you were warned about as a child. I can make it so no one ever finds a trace of you, or so your body proves as a warning to others. I have been trained in ways of torture that would make you afraid to close your eyes again."

The stench of fear hit him only seconds before the acidic, putrid smell of urine. Disgusted, Z shoved Jeb away from him again. He'd made his point. "I think we understand one another."

One by one, he glared at each dominant until they either glanced away or showed their submission. Once secure none would challenge him, Z turned his back. A part of him hoped one had the balls to approach, or at the very least to pick a fight. Testosterone still pumped hard through his veins, and Jeb's buckling did nothing to appease his craving for justice or blood. How that idiot had ever become Alpha would forever be a mystery.

The soft, gentle touch of his mate pulled him from his anger and settled his inner wolf. "Z, not one of these coyotes is worth your energy."

"Certainly not worth giving them any energy I could be giving to you." He still bristled and although she soothed him, he didn't dare return it, not while still wound tight. Never had an encounter been so personal or emotional for him, and he didn't know yet how to handle the emotions running through him. Instead, he stalked toward the forest's edge.

"We have your back, Z," one of the twins called.

They really did, and sometimes, when he'd spent years on his own and out of touch with everyone close to him, he forgot that. What he ought to do was take a quick course in togetherness, but right then he had to run—fast and hard.

He shifted, vaguely hearing Ripley ask how he could do it so quickly, before bolting for the trees. He'd gone a good sixty yards before she gained on him, nipping at his flank. Pushing harder, he ran, but she knew the land better than he did. A second later, she tackled him, rolling him into the grass.

He pinned her beneath him, and she nipped at him, her blue eyes full of playfulness. Jumping away, he gave her the chance to dart away, and dart she did, obviously wanting him to give chase. His mate could have let him run it off by himself but was giving him an outlet for his frustration. His first wife would have let him go, but Ripley, as a part of his soul, understood exactly what it would take to ease his beast.

Her silver fur shone like a beacon under the moonlight, calling to him like a lighthouse on a foggy night. He tore hard through the woods, letting the wind blow the stink of the coyotes away until he smelled only the fresh night air and his mate as she left her scent for him to follow.

For the first time in a great many years, he felt alive. Coming to an open field, he stopped in his tracks. Her silver wolf, in the midst of her shift, caused his heart to skip. He hated to see the wretched pain on her beautiful face, but it soon changed to peace in the light of the moon. With every step he made, she removed a piece of clothing.

She stood fully and gloriously naked before he made it to her side. Every inch of her, sweet perfection.

He held his shift—his human side screamed to be with her, his wolf demanded he claim her. Rubbing his fur against her skin, he marked her body fully with his scent. Only then did he shift. And while it might be quick, his ability to strip was not as fast as hers.

"Let me." She bit her lip while yanking his black T-shirt from the waistband of his jeans. Taking each piece of clothing off with painstaking slowness, she learned and caressed every inch of him until he stood before her as naked as she.

Placing her palm over his heart, she gazed into his eyes. "I thank the goddess for bringing you to me."

"I hope you feel that way when I'm gone for weeks at a time."

"By then I might be grateful for the distance."

He heard the hesitation in the words. She wouldn't handle his absence well, and he'd have to ensure the first few were short stints. Her need for physical touch grew far stronger than he would have imagined. His first wife, T, had never had an issue going a year without them seeing each other. But, Z already understood what he'd felt for her paled in comparison to the new desires surging through him for his mate. He'd adored T, but on the level of a friend who'd happened to be a lover.

Ripley's voice filled with awe. "Your heart is beating along with mine."

He covered her hand with his. "How much did your father tell you about being mated?"

"Not much. My mother was the last mated female in our pack. The few that are married now have done so because they're in love. But the pack was dying out long before my mother passed. My father was the last strong Alpha born to the pack. We breed strong betas, but recently no dominants."

Z lowered them to the soft grass, tugging her into his arms. He lay back, and she draped across him. Staring at the stars, he let a few minutes of silence pass. "Beautifully strong women. What are the numbers of your pack?"

"Seventeen betas, eight omegas, and twenty-one, no, make that twenty-two children." He heard the smile in her voice as she remembered the newest member of her family.

"I want you to head to Los Lobos with me when I approach Drew, and I want you to answer any question he has honestly."

"But...."

Z maneuvered her so she was forced to meet his eyes. She had to understand the importance of trusting

Drew. "He is the exact wolf to help your pack. And Lord knows, they could use the services of Will's cooking in his town."

Ripley stared at him and nodded before laying her head back on his chest. "What if he says no?"

Z couldn't say anything because he wouldn't force or blackmail Drew into taking on the Greystones. That would be of no use to either pack and detrimental to all the good Drew could do. Z could only hope the Alpha would take them under his wing. If Drew couldn't take them in, Z would have to find one to fill the very real urgency of her pack. He could bring Ripley back to his but none of the other members, making his dilemma a tricky one. He'd never hedged his bets all in one place, yet he'd also never walked into a meeting with more on the line.

Ripley pushed away from him, her hair cascading over her shoulder. "Z?"

He ran his fingers through her locks. "I'll make sure your pack is taken care of as if they were my own. I will find you an Alpha."

"But not you?"

He should have known she wouldn't let that go. "Not me."

"Is there anything I can do to change your mind?"

Climbing over him, she ground her pelvis into his groin.

His cock came to full alert, and he groaned. "You can try." Gripping her hips, he encouraged her to continue the friction between them.

She leaned over him, her breasts brushing against his chest. Keeping her lips a hairsbreadth away, she lifted her hips enough to allow her to reach between them and guide him into her. "Oh, I am good at the convincing thing."

He had no doubt she was, but his time for talking had ended, and he only wanted to feel. Claiming her mouth, he let her do all the convincing she wanted.

Chapter Six

Z and Ripley strolled into town and headed straight for the barn. Security, though well aware of their presence, had not stopped them but would undoubtedly run to Ryker to let him know. Whether the Enforcer felt required to join them, Z would know soon enough.

He marched into Drew's office, having left Ripley out in the hall in order for him to speak with the Alpha first. He didn't want anyone to feel put on the spot. He respected Drew too much to ambush him. Although, he hid his scent, only to hide his mated status, Z didn't get into wolf form, nor did he apply any of his stealth tactics.

"Z, I have no idea what test you're working me through." Drew threw his pencil on the desk and tipped back in his chair. "But now you're simply strolling into town with Ripley Greystone?"

"No test."

"Have a seat." Drew waited to continue until he sat. "I didn't expect you back this soon. You haven't been gone a week."

"The issues with the Greystones were pretty cut-and-dried." Z was being vague, but Ripley would do much of the explaining, not him. "I think you should hear her out again."

"Without more information, I still can't help them."

"She's willing to give you all the information you ask for."

"In your usual ambiguous manner, Z, can you at least tell me something?"

He nodded and leaned forward, resting his elbows on his knees. "Drew, the Greystones are in need of your protection. They have no Alpha, and I do believe you are the one who can fill that role."

Drew took a deep breath, focusing his attention on the ceiling. "I see."

They sat in silence, Z waiting patiently as Drew processed that information. Taking in another pack while still building his own back to health might seem a bit more than he could take on.

Finally, Drew said, "Bring Ripley in, please."

"There's something else you should know, but I don't want you to let it alter your decision," Z said, moving toward the door. Only when he opened it and motioned for Ripley to enter did he release his scent.

"You mated." Drew's response gave nothing away.

"I believe you have met my mate, Ripley." Z guided her to the chair he'd recently vacated and stood behind her, massaging her shoulders in a gentle, reassuring manner.

Drew missed nothing, and from experience, he deduced more necessary information every second. "Hello, Ripley."

"Alpha Tao," she replied, lowering her gaze out of respect.

"I understand you want me as Alpha of your pack."

"No." She lifted her chin high.

"Z?" Drew glanced at his Infiltrator.

At the same time, Z groaned. "Ripley."

"I want Z as our Alpha, but he refused." She looked at her mate before returning her attention to Drew.

"Repeatedly," Z agreed dryly.

Drew linked his fingers behind his head and smiled. "And in case you don't quite understand, Ripley, your mate will never, ever agree to be your Alpha."

"That's what he said."

"Repeatedly," Z said again and squeezed her

shoulder, gently urging her to keep going.

"So, because your first choice can't take on the role, you have come to ask me as a last resort." Drew lifted his hand when Z began to protest. "Ripley, the last time you were here, you asked for my help but refused to offer me any information to make an intelligent decision. Z assures me you're now willing to tell me what you couldn't before."

"I am." She drew in a steadying breath. "Z assures me you are nothing like your father. But it's your father who had my pack going into hiding to begin with."

That seemed to get Drew's attention. His eyes brows lifted in interest. "My father did a lot of damage, and his reach seems to grow daily. Continue, please."

"My father feared for the pack and my sisters. Your father had made a move years ago to take control. Then one of his men saw my younger sister and got it into his head he had to have her. Unfortunately, there were no strong males in our pack. Tons of betas, but we were in need of fresh, strong blood."

"And your father had heard mine had gone crazy."

She nodded. "We have been in hiding ever since. Until—"

"Until a coyote got into his head she should be

his," Z said.

"I take it the coyote situation in no longer an issue?" Drew asked Z, without an ounce of doubt in his eyes.

"Not for anyone in the Black Hills area. They're relocating to Yellowstone."

"Ouch."

"Exactly."

For the next fifteen minutes, Drew asked questions and Ripley answered them honestly and completely. She gave him the numbers and what they could bring to his pack, mainly strong women, talented omegas, and a large influx of cash. But the culinary talents of Will seemed to spark the most interest in the Alpha. And Z fed on that hunger by giving him a bite-by-bite review of the meals he'd eaten at the campsite.

Drew, unable to take the slow torture Z dished out, finally raised his palms in surrender. "What will you do if I can't take on their pack?"

Z met the other man's gaze. "I will keep searching for someone to protect them. They are my family now."

Drew nodded and turned his chair to face the window. "Stay the night. I can't say dinner will be anything worthwhile, but I'll have an answer for you in the morning."

Z thanked him and escorted Ripley out. Once they were away from the barn, she shook off his arm.

"He isn't going to take us in, is he?"

"You don't know that. He'll want to talk it over with Gee and his Enforcer. Trust me, his caution is what makes him a great Alpha. Stop worrying. Even if he doesn't take you on as your leader, the man won't leave your pack unprotected."

They walked into the bar, which had started to get a makeover while he'd been gone. The usual silence did greet him this time, but only because at that time of day everyone was out working, leaving the bar empty.

"Do you have that jar of honey your sister bottled for us before we left yesterday?"

"Yes." Ripley dug into her bag and handed him the mason jar of golden honey.

"Stay here for a second." Z kissed her nose and approached the bar. Pushing the jar across the worn surface, he laughed when the bear grabbed it just before it hit the edge.

"No label," Gee said with a smile. "But then, I knew where you were this time. Apparently, you found more than you bargained for."

"More than I thought waited for me," Z admitted.

"Well, don't leave her standing there like a lost

pup." Gee waved her over, lowering his voice so only Z could hear. "You didn't tell her about my, um...you know."

"Honey addiction? No, I didn't." Z did his best to hide his smirk, but the bear caught it.

Ignoring Z, Gee smiled and greeted his guest. "Ah, Ripley of Greystone Pack, I take it."

"Ripley, this is Gee."

She smiled and sniffed. "You're a bear."

"Last I checked. But don't hold it against me."

Z pulled a stool over and watched Gee do his best to get information from her. To his great delight, she was Z's perfect match, elusive and able to talk the bear in circles until the big guy finally huffed and waved them off before asking if Z wanted a bigger room.

"Why?" Z asked.

"I can't imagine why. You know where everything is." Lifting his chin, Gee gestured over his shoulder.

With a hand on her waist, Z guided her upstairs.

Running a finger along the dusty railing, she turned to him. "How long have you been living here?"

"Living would be a strong word. I sleep here in between assignments." He paused only long enough to grab clean linens from the closet before ushering her down the hall. "I would say I have stayed here a total of maybe twenty-five nights. I pretty much come in, stay the night, and am gone again just a quickly."

Even with exhaustion coming over him, he had the sense to check that all his charms were intact and his room undisturbed. Using the age-old chants of his people, he waited until the soft glow beckoned him in. He opened the door and motioned for her to enter before following her in. "This might be why he asked if you wanted a larger room." He let his gaze follow hers toward the twin bed in the corner. Walking over to the window, he chanted again before brushing away the remaining charms.

"We don't take up more than that when we sleep anyway." She shrugged. "Not that we've done any real sleeping together yet."

So far, they'd only slept in one position; him on his back and her curved into his side. And if he had anything to do with it, that would be the only way they would ever sleep. Still not having had a good night's sleep, he rubbed his palm across his face, suddenly bone-tired.

He yanked his shirt over his head then threw the flat sheet over the bare mattress. "I am absolutely exhausted."

Reaching out, she ran her fingers over his arm

until her hand held his. "When did you last sleep? I mean really sleep?"

"Three weeks. No, four now."

She stepped away, grabbed the fitted sheet, and remade the bed. "You have to sleep. Get in."

In between yawns, he asked, "What will you do? It's probably best not to stroll too far."

"I'll read a book I bought at the gas station we stopped at." She pulled out the romance book from her backpack and wagged it at him. "You can sleep, and I'll make sure you're safe."

He wanted to harrumph or argue he would always be the protector, but something inside him relaxed. Since he'd been a teen, no one had ever made sure he was safe when he slept. As exhaustion washed over him, a strange warm awareness of security surrounded him.

***

The knock on the door broke her away from the moment in the book where the heroine would tell the hero her big secret. Long past due, in Ripley's opinion, but now that the heroine was, Ripley didn't want to be disturbed by anyone other than her mate, whom she could not get enough of. She let her gaze move over his sleeping form. Until three hours earlier, he'd been a light sleeper, opening an eye at every noise.

Originally, she'd read in a chair across the room, but recognized his whole demeanor relaxed when she touched him. So, she'd repositioned her chair closer and ran her fingers through his hair until she heard the signs of deep sleep in his light snore. With everything he did for her pack, giving him a restful sleep seemed the least she could do.

A second knock, a bit louder, brought her from her musings. Placing the book on a table, Ripley headed for the door. Assuming it would be a wolf-shifter or perhaps the bear, she didn't bother to announce her approach. They would already know, and the less sound, the better. She wanted Z to sleep as long as possible.

Cracking the door, she was surprised to see Drew on the other side. "Alpha Tao?" She opened to door a little wider.

"Can you talk, or do you want to wait until Sleeping Beauty comes to?" Drew grinned, nodding at Z's sleeping form.

Ripley stepped out into the hall, closing the door behind her. "Z hasn't slept in weeks. I'd rather he get some rest."

"It's good to see you're taking care of him. Someone should make sure he takes a break now and then." Drew indicated they step away from the door.

The rumble of conversation drifted from the dining area, but she wasn't going to leave Z. Ripley had promised to look over him while he slept, and so she would. He'd warned her the food wouldn't be what she had been used to, so she'd packed some in her bag, and other than the few times she'd left to use a restroom, she had remained been by his side.

"I would prefer to stay here."

"Fair enough." Leaning against the railing, Drew crossed his arms, then one leg over the other. "I talked with my Enforcer and Gee. I didn't want you to have to wait till morning for my decision."

"I appreciate that." Her stomach lurched as nerves engulfed her much like they had the first day she had approached the Toa Alpha.

"I wish you had been more open with me during our initial meeting." He raised a palm, halting anything she might have said in her defense. "But, I understand why you couldn't. My own pack still has a hard time with trust, so why shouldn't I expect that from surrounding packs? That being said, I can't be completely sorry you weren't, because if you had been, I wouldn't have sent Z and he wouldn't have found his mate."

Ripley felt the same. Although the idea someone would send a spy into her camp to get information about her still irked her. The outcome had worked to her advantage, though. As Drew had said, she'd found her mate and her pack had been rid of their nemesis, the coyotes. Now, the future of her pack lay in the hands of the man before her.

"I have been locked in my office since you left me this morning. I've discussed your request with my Enforcer, whose concern is he doesn't know enough about your pack to overstretch an already shaky one. Gee believes we should focus on building our own before branching out. My mate thinks a pack of strong betas might cause inner chaos within the betas already fighting for the dominant males' attention."

Life would be so easy if Z would just take on the position as Alpha. Ripley nodded. "I understand. As soon as Z awakens, I'll have him escort me to my pack." A hand on her elbow stopped her from turning away completely.

"I'm not done yet. Those were the cons, but there were pros, too. Ryker doesn't trust Z because he can't swear his loyalty to me or the pack. That, and Z's whole reason to exist is to prove he can sneak past security and get the information he is after without anyone knowing."

"He told me on the way here if he can get through, anyone can, but if he can't, no one will."

"Exactly. But Ryker believes if you are a member who has sworn allegiance to the Tao Pack, then Z has a more vested interest in the pack's longevity. Gee agrees with Z that I am the Alpha for you and we in turn can use you." Drew paused. "Of course, some of that could be because Gee wants the history he doesn't have on your pack, and the thought this Will could come in and teach his cooks something makes all our mouths water. Finally, and personally, the most important person to bend my ear, my mate, Betty, believes although there will be issues between some of the betas, having strong women who are equally strong in business could give the other betas an incentive to venture out. Did I mention this Will guy?"

The comic break allowed Ripley to relax. "You did, and trust me he is amazing."

"Are you prepared and able to swear loyalty to me as your Alpha for yourself and, by proxy, for your pack?"

"I am."

"Good. In the morning, you and Z come to the barn and we will make it official. Each of your pack will have to do so in person when they are able. It can wait until off-season, but I don't believe even with Z's presence and that of his twin brothers, your pack can wait for me to give you my protection. You're too rich in resources and betas. Besides, coyotes are too stupid to keep their mouths shut."

"I thank you on behalf of all the Greystone."

"I was supposed to invite you and Z to join us for dinner, but I'll send your regrets to Betty."

After a few more minutes of discussion, Drew excused himself. Ripley entered the room, now filled with soft, muted moonlight. She opened the window, allowing the crisp night air to fill her lungs. With the safety of her pack assured, some of the tension she has been carrying around eased and hope entered. Stripping naked, she climbed into the bed between Z and the wall. His arm snaked around her, securing her to his side. Sleep found her quickly in the secure embrace of her mate.

Epilogue

Four months later....

Ripley placed the last of the river rafts into storage. Another season behind them and, for the first time, she looked forward to some time away from the water.

Rubbing her belly, she smiled. "You, little one, will love the river."

"You, Mama, shouldn't be handling those rafts by yourself." The deep, familiar voice of her mate rumbled through her.

Turning, she threw herself at Z, and he lifted her into his arms. "When did you arrive?"

Walking them toward the office, he caught her lips with his. Three weeks had been too long and, having only two days between a two-and-a-half week mission for his pack and a three-week one for Drew, she'd missed her man.

She ran her hands along his chest and under his T-shirt, hissing as her power surged. "We aren't doing this in your office again."

"That's what you said last time."

Once inside, he lowered her to her feet. "Where is everyone, and why aren't they helping you close shop? And why didn't you wait for me to do this?"

"One question at a time, spy king. Everyone is packing for their trip to Los Lobos. Will is so excited about catering this party Drew is allowing us to throw to thank the Taos, he has everyone running around to find the right ingredients."

"The Taos will be happy with anything that isn't made of hamburger, trust me. So, why didn't you wait?"

"Because I didn't think you would return before we left. It's not as if you punch a timecard and can ask for days off. I understood this when I signed on." And once Ripley had gotten past the incessant desire to touch him, the arrangement worked well for her. She had her freedom to run the rafting company and the tours as she wished, and when Z came into town, he either joined her tours or she took time off. "Besides, the rafts are hardly that heavy."

"What if a human stumbled along? No human woman could lift that raft on her own. You have to be more careful, and I am not even going to talk about the fact you're pregnant and Janey has already warned you about heavy lifting." Placing his open palm against her belly, Z pressed gently. "I don't want either of you hurt."

"We're fine now that you're here."

"Lock up and let's get to the compound. I'm sure Will has plenty to keep us both busy. I can help you finish winterizing around here after the loyalty ceremony with Drew."

"You're coming back even after meeting with Drew?"

"I'm here for a couple weeks before we have to make an appearance with my Alpha together."

She stopped in her tracks. "Wait. You're taking me to your pack? I thought it was a big no-no."

"Apparently, the realization our baby might have Infiltrator powers made them rethink their position. I figure it will take those two weeks to help you prepare for the meeting. The twins have asked to stay on after the pack returns here, so I have sent in a plea for that, as well. I thought again using the baby might get us all what we want."

Ripley locked the door behind them and held his hand as they walked to the SUV. When he helped her into the front seat, she paused. "You know I have already sworn my allegiance to the Alpha. I'm not really needed there."

Z's eyes darkened with desire. "But everyone else has to be there."

"That's what I love about you. That brain of yours worked right through the heart of a problem." She lowered his head so she could caress his neck with her lips.

"I still have to see your Alpha."

Between kisses, she said. "Is he expecting you?"

"He's always expecting me, and at the same time, never."

"So, as long as no one sees you, and I claim a bit of morning sickness, no one will question why we aren't there."

"The camp still intact?" Z asked.

"Yes," Ripley purred into his ear.

"There still a boat upriver?"

"Affirmative."

Grabbing the cell phone he'd purchased for her before his first mission apart from her, he placed it in her hand. "Call your sister. Tell her you're going to get back to nature to appease your baby's spirit guide."

"She'll never buy it."

Tapping the phone, he said, "Make the call."

She did, and an hour later, she and her mate were lying naked in a random tent, listening to the sounds of nature around them and their own heartbeats, perfectly in time with each other. Drew had proven to be a good Alpha, and she hoped her pack would prove to be as good a gamble.

But she loved Z, and she wanted only to see him. In the end, their Alpha was a figurehead, a requirement to keep others at bay, and Z was the man who showed her how to live how to love.

And she thanked the stars he'd infiltrated her pack.

About Dominique

Award winning, bestselling author Dominique Eastwick grew up a US Navy Brat, so if there was a Naval base that was probably home. She currently resides in North Carolina with her husband, two children, crazy lab and lazy cat.

When not writing you can find Dominique behind the lens of her camera.

http://dominiqueeastwick.blogspot.com

www.ingramcontent.com/pod-product-compliance
Lightning Source LLC
Chambersburg PA
CBHW070340130626
46556CB00007B/2958